GREEN EYES

MARGUERITE DURAS

Green Eyes

Translated from the French by Carol Barko

COLUMBIA UNIVERSITY PRESS

NEW YORK

The Press is grateful to the French Ministry of Culture
for a grant assisting the preparation of this translation.

Columbia University Press
New York Oxford
Les Yeux verts copyright © Cahiers du Cinéma, 1980, 1987.
English translation copyright © 1990 Columbia University Press

Library of Congress Cataloging-in-Publication Data
Duras, Marguerite.
[Yeux verts. English]
Green eyes / Marguerite Duras ; translated from the French by
Carol Barko.
p. cm.
Translation of: Les yeux verts.
ISBN 0-231-06946-4 : $24.95
I. Title.
PQ2607.U8245Y4913 1990
844'.912—dc20
90-44461
CIP

Photo credits: AGIP, page 72; Hélène Bamberger, page 199; François Barrat,
page 118; Édouard Boubat, page 43; *Cahiers du cinéma*, pages 150, 163, 165,
178; Bertrand Clech, page 149; DR, pages 9, 17, 18, 19, 33, 36, 38, 117,
148, 199; Dimitri Fedotov, pages 64, 67; Dominique Issermann, pages 6, 71,
86; Erica Leenhardt, page 10; Dominique Le Rigoleur, pages 4, 46, 88, 103;
Jean Mascolo, pages 1, 80, 83, 102, 105, 126, 128, 138, 141, 144, 180, 186;
Pic, page 52; Vincent Pinel, page 96; Private collection, pages 19–26, 61,
69; Dominique Villain, page 173.

Printed in the United States of America
c 10 9 8 7 6 5 4 3 2 1

CONTENTS

v

vi

TRANSLATOR'S ACKNOWLEDGMENTS

I thank Bronwen Sennish for sharing with me her technical knowledge of cinema, William L. Gross for his inspired research help, and especially Danièle Lasser and Lois Meredith for their suggestions for solving problems in translation.

FOREWORD TO THE FRENCH EDITION

This new edition in book form of *Green Eyes* includes all of Marguerite Duras' texts which appeared in the June 1980 issue of *Cahiers du Cinéma*, following the author's wishes regarding page layout, in collaboration with Serge Daney who was responsible for coordinating the issue, with the assistance of Pascal Bonitzer, Michèle Manceaux, François Régnault, and Charles Tesson.

New texts and conversations, as well as additional photos, are included in this edition of *Green Eyes:* "The Tremulous Man" (a conversation between the American filmmaker Elia Kazan and the author, which appeared in *Cahiers du Cinéma* in December 1980), an article on *L'Homme Atlantique* (published in *Le Monde*, November 27, 1981, in conjunction with the release of the film), another article on Aline Isserman's film, *Juliette's Lot* (*Libération*, October 18, 1983), and finally a conversation with the author on *The Children* ("In the Gardens of Israel, It was Never Night") (*Cahiers du Cinéma*, July–August 1985).

One doesn't know in life when things are there. They escape you. You were telling me the other day that life seemed to be dubbed. That's exactly what I feel. My life is a dubbed film, badly edited, badly acted, badly adapted, in sum a mistake. A thriller with no killings, without a cop or victims, without any subject at all. It could be a real film under these conditions and no, it's false. You want to know what it would take for it to be so. For me to be on a stage saying nothing, to let myself see, without especially thinking about something. That's right.

M. D., October 1986
(*Excerpt from* La vie matérielle)

GREEN EYES

THE LETTER

The origin of *Aurélia Steiner* is a letter addressed to someone I don't know. We talk on the telephone. I know his name. I saw him once thirteen years ago. I've forgotten his face. I know his voice. I wrote this letter and then I didn't send it. With this letter, all of a sudden, I began again to write. I was going to go on to the main thing, forgetting to say this.

THE LETTER

Neauphle-le-Château
3 July 1979

I'm reading your letters. I'm keeping them.

I'm not doing anything. I hang out every night in the Yvelines cafes or at people's homes. I drink. I've agreed to do a thirty-minute film at the end of July, to write it, that is. I had promised to send you N. Night and the right version of Vera Baxter, I didn't do it. I don't know how the time goes by, I'm not doing anything. I must manage to put together those texts, Césarée, Les Mains négatives (Negative Hands), with that older text still without a title that I've been commissioned to do by the end of July. I want you to read what I'm doing, to give you fresh, new writings, fresh woes, the ones now in my life. The rest, the things lying around in the blue cabinets in my bedroom, will be published at any rate some day, either after my death or before, if ever again I'm short of money. At this moment there are ninety thousand roses in the garden and this kills me. I don't like the summer. I don't know what you're going to do in R., you tell me to go often to this city and this intrigues me. I heard you had a house on one of those islands along the shores of the Charente. I'll screen Césarée and Les Mains négatives for you between July 16 and July 20 at La Pagode cinema. In August I'll go to that Trouville apartment overlooking the sea. Some day I'll send you a key to that apartment and you'll go with your present wife. This will take place when I'm abroad, far away, so that we are assured of not meeting. You'll see, it's an apartment jutting out over the sea. When there are storms, the sound of the sea comes into the rooms in your sleep. Each time I hope to stay there longer, at least until winter, always to write. Always this. The whole time. If I don't manage to do this, I'll write you letters, I'll send them to you. Twenty letters. A hundred letters. Writing to you, for me, is writing, this by reason of what ties me to you, so violent a love. No longer can I, and you understand, write a coherent story, see it through, give it the pretext of a subject, and develop it in all its consequences, from the first ones to the last. It's over. I don't know how to say it clearly to you. I can tell you only that to reach the point of trying, for instance, to say it to you, I am forced to go through what seems like a fragmentation of the writing, of the time that structures it, and above all to constantly reshuffle the direction of its components. For instance, suddenly, to go on to this:

It's three in the afternoon, I am in this spacious room where I like to be in summer, with this forest of roses outside the windows and, for three days now, this skinny white cat who comes to look at me very closely, eye to eye, through the windows, frightens me; it's crying it's lost and it wants to stay in one spot, maybe here, and no, I don't want any more cats here since Ramona's death, the black cat, my friend, my sister, my love, whom I mourned for days when she was run over by a car exactly like mine—rumor had it that because it was a Friday evening, she'd thought I wouldn't come that evening the way I usually did every weekend. She's buried in a forest of oak and chestnut trees that now bears her name.

I would also have to go through this other white, skinny, crazy cat, disturbing, significant, through this static rose garden around this cat, through this pond which the village children have dirtied and which this year is filled with frogs and toads that these children try to stone to death, I would have to go through all this in order to reach you and to bring the two of us together, closer to the world's totality and our common despair. I am forgetting; the garden is full of birds and the white cat is going

crazy with hunger and I will give it nothing, I don't want to, there's nothing to be done.

Maybe I will do that, write you letters. And you can do with them what I'd be happy to have you do, in short, what you want. When I'm writing I'm not dying. Who would die when I write? I must not spend my nights drinking anymore, I must go to bed early so as to be able to write you very long letters in order not to die.

I could have also told you about that walk, about the cemetery in Barneville, about the children, the children's graves in the sun, about Julien who got scared and ran away and about her, the other child. And about the way back along the sea. About the beauty of the sea. Its softness. It was as if covered with the weight of that softness. With night falling, I asked myself if I would write again. It was the beginning of the summer.

4

The letters I would write you seem to me like accidental lights in the darkness of time, pinpoints in the thickness and heaviness of the days which are shrouded by the darkness even while something is always left, a shadow on the softness of the sea, a twinge, the pain at having forgotten the children's graves in the sun, the little girl, the one who was reading the writing on the child's grave, June 29, 1979, at Barneville la Bertran. Cecile was her name. Still standing in the path, deep in thought. She didn't want to leave the cemetery. All alone, diligently reading, the history of the dead children.

POLITICAL LOSS

For many people the true loss of political meaning is to join a party unit, to submit to its rule, its law. For many people, too, when they talk about an apolitical stance, they are primarily talking about an ideological loss or shortcoming. I can't speak for you, for your thoughts. For me, political loss is primarily the loss of self, the loss of one's anger as much as of one's gentleness, the loss of one's hatred, of one's faculty for hatred as much as of one's faculty for loving, the loss of one's imprudence as much as of one's moderation, the loss of excess as much as the loss of measure, the loss of madness, of one's naiveté, the loss of one's courage like one's cowardice, like that of one's horror in the face of everything as much as that of one's confidence, the loss of one's tears like one's joy. That's what I think.

6

NON-WORK

And no, not writing either, I don't think that this is work. I thought so for a long time, I don't think so anymore. I think it is non-work. *It is getting to non-work.* The text, the equilibrium of the text, is in itself a space you have to rediscover. Here I can no longer speak of economy, of form, no, but of a relationship of forces. I can't say more than this. You must manage to control what suddenly turns up. To struggle against a force that sweeps through and that you must pin down or else have it go beyond you and get lost. Or else have it destroy its disordered and irreplaceable coherence. No, to work is to create this empty space in order to allow the unforeseen, the obvious, to come. To let go, then pick up again, to retrace your steps, to be as inconsolable for having let it come as for having let it go. To remove oneself. And then sometimes, yes, to write. Everyone does, looks for these moments when one retreats from oneself, this state of being anonymous to oneself which one hides. You don't know. You know nothing about what you're doing.

More than anything else, writing attests to this unawareness of what is liable to happen when you are there, sitting at the so-called work table, of what is caused by this material fact of sitting in front of a table with whatever you need to compose letters on the still untouched page.

WHITE

Listen, I was still young, it was here in the country. In June or July, I think. There was a full moon. It was late in the evening after dinner. D. was in the garden. He called me. He told me he wanted to show me what was happening to the whiteness of the white flowers in the full moon when the weather was clear. He didn't know whether I had already noticed. In fact, I hadn't, ever. There was snow where the clumps of daisies and white roses were, but snow so bright, so white that it made the whole garden, the other flowers, the trees, dark. The red roses had become very dark, they almost disappeared. What was left was that inconceivable whiteness I have never forgotten. The night was so transparent that the sky was blue. You could have read outdoors so intense was the light. When we were children, in the full moon we would read at night on the veranda of the bungalow, facing the forest of Siam.

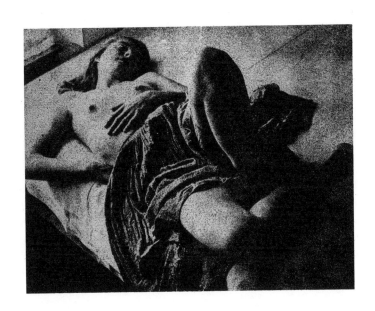

WHITE IN BLACK AND WHITE

There is no white in color films. True white, the white of snow, of foam, of white flowers on moonlit nights, is rendered only by black and white. The snow in Aurélia Steiner runs along the wharves of Vancouver in the foam of the sea, I recognized it in the film.

AURÉLIA, AURÉLIA

Aurélia. She is in the present, here, like Alissa in *Détruire (Destroy, She Said)*: they are still eighteen. The writing I rediscover with Aurélia. She is everywhere, Aurélia is, she writes from everywhere at the same time. After *Aurélia Steiner*, I can't write anymore, I lose the writing. If I don't talk with this survivor, I lose the writing.

And if she isn't there, present all the time, nighttime, daytime, to prevent me from seeing anything but her, all the rest, everything, nothing comes. I don't write. I stay closeted with Aurélia for a month and a half. I would get up, I would see Aurélia's ocean, her eyes, I would see that the ocean was crying or sleeping with Aurélia's cries or her sleep.

CLASSIFIED ADS

"The woman who, last Monday at seven in the evening, passing by the flower shop at number x on rue Tronchet, turned around to the man standing in front of the door, is requested to identify herself."

This was a classified ad in a newspaper, twenty years ago.

Some friends told me: One Saturday, at a showing of *Aurélia Steiner* at the Action-République, there was a couple behind them who had come in by chance. The man, after a minute, said: But what are we doing here, we just ran in here, it isn't the movie we wanted to see, we're leaving. And the woman said: It makes no difference to *me*, this interests me, I'm staying. And the man stayed with her. And at the end of *Aurélia Steiner Vancouver*, they were still there. I could ask this woman to identify herself. *He* would have left. *She* accepted right away this film they had probably never tried to see. She probably didn't have any bad habits yet. She still had all her curiosity.

—*You think she'll identify herself?*

They probably don't read *Cahiers.** But who knows?

I take my hat off to her. I embrace her. The people who put classified ads in the newspapers are the people in *Les Mains négatives (Negative Hands)* but they never get a response. And they don't know how to reach out. The man who placed his hands on the granite walls of the El Castillo cave, just like the man from the Bronx who writes his name and address on the walls and the subways, they don't know how to cry out, to reach out. *I'm* here for that, to know how. This is still the function I feel is mine. The path of the dolly shot cuts through this world of appeals you never see. You weren't expecting to come upon a

* *Cahiers du Cinéma*, the magazine and publisher of the French edition of this book.

11

world of garbage cans, of dumps, of blacks, of blacks. It makes me think of Harlem. Yes, that's it, like a "slice" of Harlem, at dawn, when there aren't any children, they're sleeping, almost no more women.

THE VIEWER

We must try to talk about the viewer, about the original viewer. The one we call childish, who goes to the movies to be entertained, to have a good time, and who only gets that far. This viewer is the one responsible for the older cinema. The most "educated" of all viewers. In fact, he's the one who was taught in his youth that the function of movies was to entertain, that you went in particular to forget. When this viewer, this original viewer, goes into a movie house, it's to flee what's outside, the street, the crowd, to escape himself, to enter into something else, the film, to lose the part of him concerned with work, studies, the couple, relationships, the part that is repeated every day. He has gone no further since childhood, and similarly that's where he still is, in cinematographic childhood. It's perhaps there, in the movie house, that this viewer finds his only solitude and this solitude consists of turning from himself. When he's ready to give himself to the cinema, the film takes charge of him, it does with him, in fact, what *it* wants. It's there that the viewer rediscovers the unlimited hold that sleep and childhood play have on him. This viewer is both the most numerous, the youngest, and the most irreducible in every country in the world. He has the constancy of childhood. Everywhere it's the same. He wants to keep his old toy, his old movie, his empty fort. He keeps it. This viewer is part of the greatest number, he is the unchanged, unchangeable majority of all time, the majority in wars and right-wing votes, the one that runs through history whose very object it is, the completely unaware majority. It behaves the same way with cinema. Mute, neutral, it does not comment, it does not judge the movies it sees. It goes to the movies or it doesn't.

This viewer is roughly the whole blue-collar population, but also many scientific types, many technicians, many people whose work is highly specific. The scientific types are in the majority: the technological population, the mathematicians, all the managers, the whole building trade. Starting from the bricklayers, the engineers, the plumbers, the foremen, to the promoters.

"The youth of the labor force," say those who govern us. "The laboring population," say the others. The ones who have an education, or those who do not, find themselves on equal standing in the same movie house. The ones who have studied medicine, physics, film, the ones who have only studied the sciences, whose studies never diverged from the main track, never with anything to vary them, find themselves with those who have had a technical education or no education at all. Along with these people you must consider the vast majority of critics, those who validate the choice of the original viewer, who sanction "personal" films and defend action films adapted to everyone's taste, and who show such hatred for *le cinéma d'auteur* that you can't avoid seeing here as well a suppressed anger, but of a source other than what is offered as a pretext. For all these people, one goes to movies to rediscover the thing that makes one laugh, the thing that will while away the time, the constancy of the childish game, the violence of wars, of massacres, of riots, virility in all its forms, the virility of fathers, of mothers, from every angle, the good old laughs on women, the cruelties, the sex life of others. The only tragedies, here, are

1 3

about love or jockeying for power. All the movies this viewer will see are parallel, they always go in the same direction, always with the same expectation of how events will unfold, and be resolved. When this viewer walks out on a film before the end, it is because the film has demanded an effort of readjustment, an adult effort to reach its level. Now what he wanted was not to view but to review movies.

This viewer is separate from us, from me. I know I will never reach him and I do not try to reach him. I know who he is. I know that nothing can change him, that he is unreachable. We are unreachable. We are face to face, in a permanent separateness. By himself he will never stand for the total population. We will always be there, on the fringe, we who write, we who create books, movies. This viewer you cannot name, you don't know what to call him, so you don't. It doesn't matter. Whatever name you give him, it doesn't matter. The way things are is that in the city, in the mob of the city, we are two. There is me and there is him and neither of us will ever approach the other. Our rights are strictly equal to theirs; my right is equal to his. We are of equal standing. Yes. Our right to survive in the city is the same. If I am fewer in numbers, I am just as inevitable, just as irreducible. As time goes by, in decades and decades, will he ever finally understand that he isn't the only one? I don't think so. I don't see how this viewer would manage to escape the trap of his own predominance, maintained the way he is in child-hood by the whole ruling ideology, official or para-official. He makes the city work. We don't make anything work, we are simply there, at the same time as he, in the city.

These viewers refer to themselves as "we." "We the young," "we the workers." I say I: "I who make films, difficult or not, they're films." What I'm saying is what I observe happening between him and me. What I'm saying right now about the viewer is what I think of our encounter. I cannot make a judg-

14

ment that would boast of having him stand for the general way of thinking. I still don't see how one could address the theoretical or critical position of this original viewer. He comes from a place that seems unreal, deserted, dead, killed by a mad scramble, of individuals running from themselves. Yes, a kind of immoral position. To speak of him in the name of all, you can only do from a position of like immorality.

My viewers range between fifteen and forty thousand. This is the figure for my novel *Le Ravissement de Lol V. Stein (The Ravishing of Lol V. Stein)* in the Blanche series. It's a lot. The figure for the paperback edition must be sixty thousand but the number or readers must be the same: thirty to forty thousand. A lot of people keep the book and don't get around to reading it, don't take the trouble to get into it, the way they do for films. I'm saying that it's an important figure. I'm saying that these are important figures, for a book the same as for a film. There's no getting away from it. Professional filmmakers count viewers in terms of weight. I have a feeling that the young filmmakers are inconsolable at not going beyond the thirty-thousand-people mark. You're afraid that they've gotten to the point of doing anything to reach the three-hundred-thousand mark, to catch up with that figure, the one that ruins, and that will ruin them. Let them drown in it, all together, the filmmakers and these original viewers. We are separate. What would it mean to get them on our side? Nothing. Win them over to no purpose since what we would be doing then would no longer make any sense as far as we're concerned. In what terms could we address them? We don't know their language and they don't know ours. This difference between them and us is akin to the great wastelands in history. Between them and us there is history, the plagues of political history, their long drawn-out repercussions. Yes, that's what it's really about, about that wasteland, about those hopeless stretches of time-honored repetition, the same repeated attempt to see and to understand one another. Here, all is vanity and whistling in the wind.

You can't ever force a child to read. The child who is punished because he's reading the comics will perhaps stop reading them, but he will never by command move on to other readings. Or else you indoctrinate him, with the worst result of all. In Hitler Germany, in Soviet Russia, there are only dogmatic films. The effect of this is the worst of all. We only have to see what the unconditional obedience of the troops and the staff of the P.C.F.* has produced, that leveling of intelligence, that dreadful turning of the individual into his corpse. This has given us the young indoctrinated Nazis or Soviets, the young soldiers of Prague and Kabul. You can't ever make someone see what he hasn't seen himself, discover what he hasn't discovered alone. Never without destroying his view, *his* view, whatever he does with it.

This viewer, I think, we must leave to himself. If he must change, he'll change, like everyone, all at once or slowly from words overheard in the street, from being in love, from something he's read, from someone he's met, but alone. In a solitary confrontation with change.

* The French Communist Party.

16

17

Paris, 13 octobre 1977.

Madame,

Si vous désiriez savoir ce qu'est devenue la jeune femme (Anne-Marie Stretter) qui vous plaisait à Saïgon, venez assister à la causerie qu'elle fera, à 8 ans, dans sa maison de retraite, le 26 octobre à 17¹⁷30 (3 bis rue du Bel-Air, 92 MEUDON-BELLEVUE).

C'est ma grand'mère ; après vous avoir entendue à la télévision et vu India Song, nous lui avons parlé de vous. C'est elle qui m'a suggéré de vous inviter. A bientôt, j'espère.

Odile Le Roy

21

Le Châtelet
3 bis rue du Bel Air
92190 Meudon — Bellevue
15 mai 22

Madame,

Vous avez raison de rester
silencieuse —

À travers la jeune femme que j'étais,
votre imagination a créé une image
fictive et p... grand son charme
grâce justement à cet anonymat
mystérieux et p.t faut préserver —
J'en suis si profondément convaincue
moi-même, que je n'ai voulu ni lire
votre livre, ni voir votre film —
Discrétion de souvenirs, d'impressions
qui gardent leur valeur à rester
dans l'ombre, dans la conscience
du réel devenu irréel ——

Vieilly après, je vous prie l'expression de mes sentiments les meilleurs

L. Striedter

23

24

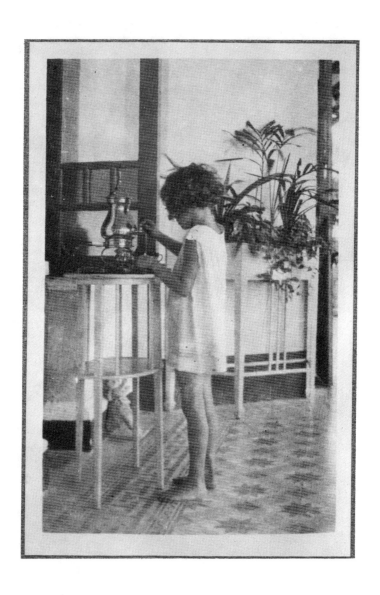

I WANTED TO TELL YOU

I wanted to tell you, if I were young, if I were eighteen, if I knew nothing yet about the separation between people and the nearly mathematical permanence of this separation between people, I would do the same as now, I would do the same books, make the same movies. In other words, I wanted to tell you that I have remained eighteen like them, those readers, those original viewers. If I had died yesterday I would have been dead at eighteen. If I die in ten years I will also have died at eighteen.

I tell you, too, we think we can't survive knowing those abominable facts of the hopeless separation between people. Now, it isn't true. You survive it. You can. You can do it your own way.

Before, when I was still young, I thought, at least that's what I said, that among the horrible facts of this knowledge, I could only live at that point where memory and forgetfulness meet. Not remembering, not having forgotten. Now I think that these words, dictated to me by the men I've known, are meaningless, that they come from the immensity of a general folly, a shadowy place, the way we become obedient to power, the way people are intimidated by the deadly irresponsibility of the proletariat, and that these words were invented to conceal the dazzling temptation of the only acceptable behavior of nations with regard to the power governing them, wherever it comes from, whatever its nature, and with regard to that soured hope in the redemptive and constructive vision of the proletariat; I'm speaking of what is not in the nature of things that may be taught, that escape all classification, any kind of schooling, that can neither be counseled nor made learnable; I'm speaking of indifference. The new grace of a heaven without God.

I REMEMBER

I remember August 6, 1945. My husband and I were in a deportees' home near Lake Annecy. I read the newspaper headline on the Hiroshima bomb. Then I rushed out of the boarding-house and I leaned against the wall facing the road, as if suddenly I'd fainted standing up. Little by little I returned to my senses, I recognized life, the road. It was the same in 1945 while the German charnel houses in the concentration camps were being discovered. I would station myself in railroad stations and in front of hotel entrances with photos of my husband and my friends and I would wait without any hope for the survivors' return, in a state close to the one I'd been in at Annecy. I wasn't weeping, outwardly I was the same as ever except that I could no longer talk at all. These are very exact, very clear memories; I had clearly become another person. Later, and this is what I'm getting to, later on in my life, I never wrote on the war, on those moments, never anymore, except a few pages, on the concentration camps. Similarly, if I had not been commissioned to do Hiroshima, I would not have written anything on Hiroshima either and when I did, you see, I compared the enormous number of the Hiroshima deaths with the story of the death of a single love that I had invented. I could write *Le Ravissement de Lol V. Stein* in a country put to fire and the sword. I could also write *Le Vice-Consul (The Vice-Consul)* everywhere, in Cuba, in Kabul, yes, that's right. But not in Russia. There I can't write.

YOU, THE OTHER, IN OUR SEPARATION

While I speak, while I write these things, I know they will not in any way matter to you, the other, in our separation, if by chance, some day, you should be reading something besides *L'Équipe* and *Le Parisien*, for instance. But you see, you don't matter anymore to me now either. One cannot live off the dead. Nor do I hear anymore your tight-lipped silence like the silence of those who govern us. I left you. For a long time now, a very long time, I have kept the despair caused by you through negligence. It has become illegible and sterile dust. The people who are still affected by your irresponsibility, your dishonesty, I see as victims of a seasonal malady which will pass. Yes, your existence has the same effect as the end of desire, that frightening expiration of a dying desire which no force in the world, however tremendous, can bring back to life for the space of a look. But you see, I call you nevertheless, I write to you nevertheless, as I would have done at eighteen. Similarly, I would call you, would write to you if you suddenly disappeared or were struck dead; you never know, given the history of your class. The distance separating us is indeed that of death. It is one and the same distance for you and for me. Just as *you* want to keep it pure between us, *I* cover it by shouting and calling. Like you, I know this distance is insurmountable, impossible to cover. The difference between you and me is that for me this impossibility is a minor drawback. So you see, we are similar, we both similarly stay in our respective compartments, in our scorched, incalculably narcissistic territories, but *I* shout *toward* the deserts, preferably in the direction of the deserts.

MAKING MOVIES

I don't know how I fit into the cinema. I've made movies. For professionals, the movies I make do not exist. Losey, in his book, praises my texts and condemns my movies to death; he says he hates *Détruire dit-elle (Destroy, She Said)*. For me, he has never made a movie that can hold a candle to *Détruire dit-elle*.

This proves that my movies cannot cross the professionals' border either. And, similarly, that theirs can no longer cross mine. I had started out by seeing their movies and then I made mine and they counted less and less. By professionals, I mean people who make reproductions of movies the way others turn out reproductions of paintings, as opposed to authors who write for cinema, to artists who paint paintings. The world of that kind of cinema is filled with driven people; it's the preserve of fear, fear of missing the chance to film, of missing millions, billions. For that cinema world, we are offenders who take "their" money. Someone—I don't know who—recently said on television, an angry man: "The effect of giving money to Duras to film *Le Camion (The Truck)* is to turn off movie audiences for six months." What praise. It's true, I enjoyed it. But that man was mistaken. I never had an advance for *Le Camion*. In literature, you can't say: I'm just 220 million short of finishing my book. If the book isn't done, even under the worst conditions, it means that it isn't to be done. If it must be done, it will be done even under the worst conditions of adversity. The excuses for not writing, the time that's lacking, the too many things you have to do, etc., aren't true, almost never. The same necessity doesn't hold for filmmakers. They look for subjects. That, too, is one of the decisive differences. They look for stories. They get proposals, either novels or scripts done by specialists of their genre. Often. They appraise these proposals, tally them up: three crimes, one cancer, one love, plus such and such an actor. Result: 700,000 viewers. The whole thing goes on the computer. The movie is made. Result: 600,000 viewers. A failure.

The mass-market filmmakers who succeed on a massive scale —twenty-five movie houses, a million and a half viewers—have a *strange longing* for our movies, the ones they have never tackled, the ones that aren't validated by profit, the money-making failures—only one movie house, ten thousand tickets sold. They would like *at the same time* to take our place, to replace us in addition to what they do, to take those ten thousand viewers from us, as if they could. And we in no way would like to replace them; we wouldn't know how to do it besides. We coexist with them as we do with the original viewer; we have equal rights to theirs. Whereas we are the symbol of commercial failure, students do more dissertations on us than on them, and sometimes publications like this one also acknowledge our existence. Despite the efforts made by the daily press not to know about us, we continue to make movies. This the mass-market cinema cannot bear. Whereas *we* forget it. Yes, there is here a strange and new longing for the failure which sets itself up as the equal of free choice. This longing represents some improvement for the mass-market filmmaker, even if it passes through anger and insult directed at us. Money is not the sole object anymore, not entirely. Nor are the number of seats. Something else is beginning to emerge, admittedly still a long way off; a sense of the inanity of the movie-making profit that leaves its maker so alone, that deserts him as soon as it happens, and also another feeling which itself relates to the very person, to his responsibility toward himself. Some young mass-market filmmakers have even stopped doing us harm, speaking ill of us, and are themselves also trying to come under the umbrella of *le cinéma d'auteur*, claiming to be both auteur and general interest at the same time, but successful. Tavernier.

I recall Raymond Queneau saying that in France only certain readers, two to three thousand readers, would decide the fate of a book, and depending on whether these readers—the most demanding of all—would or would not remember certain titles, those titles would or would not take their place in French literature. And that if you did not have those readers, no audience, even if very wide, could take their place. For cinema, you can talk about 10,000 viewers who make the films and who, sticking to their guns in the face of all opposition, establish their reputation in cinema or throw them out. This margin of 2,000 to 10,000 viewers, most mass-market filmmakers never have. They may have two million viewers but in those ten million you won't find these same two to ten thousand viewers who are ours.

GODARD

Last year Godard asked me to appear in a short sequence of his film, which at the time was called *Sauve qui peut (la vie)* *(Every Man for Himself)*. I didn't want to be in it but only to have an interview with him. So he asked me to come. I went. This was in October 1979, in Lausanne. He told me that the whole thing was set up, the time and the places for our interview. He took me into a school, at recreation time or at the reopening of the school, I don't know which anymore; it was beneath a wooden staircase that the schoolchildren used. So we did the interview. I didn't understand a thing he was saying to me. He didn't understand a thing I was saying to him, not only because of the infernal noise in the school, but no matter, it amounted to an interview. At the end he laughed and said to me: "To think I made you come from Paris to talk in this place."

After that we knew each other better, it seems to me, and I felt a definite friendship for him. It would seem that up to then he and I had had opposite problems in film, especially in the text/image relationship. But who knows, maybe not, it also depends on how he would put it, if he were to put it. After the school we recorded in a car, but a moving one, riding through the city. I listened to the tape. It would seem that from time to time, at the red lights, you can pretty well understand what is being said. It seemed to me, too, that there were some interesting things about the overhead footbridges in Lausanne that go from one building to the other. I told him they were beautiful. He told me that a lot of people were throwing themselves off those footbridges. I said they seemed to have been purposely made to kill oneself. He said yes.

WOODY ALLEN CHAPLIN

I saw *Annie Hall* last night in order to keep up somewhat with you people at *Cahiers du Cinéma* who are so up on things in film. Right off I was quite charmed; that's the word, I found it charming, and then it vanished. The next morning, there was nothing left. I think that Woody Allen, an unknown for me only a few days ago, is illustrative of a very contrived art, and similarly of a very local humor, meticulously perfected, not nearly as vast —much less so—as Chaplin's. Woody Allen is only where he is. Nothing changes around him, things stay different, they don't take off with him. He doesn't modify anything. The New York you see around him is the same. He goes through New York, and New York is the same. Chaplin's space, in *City Lights*, is completely filled by him. Wherever Chaplin is, in New York or somewhere else, everything reverberates with him after he's been there. Everything is Chaplin's. The whole city, cities, streets. Everything belongs to Chaplin after he's been there. To this man, who doesn't say a word. With Chaplin there is only one number, one act, as it were: only one appearance, one silence, one love. This act takes place in an equally unique place but an immense one. The place belongs entirely to him. Chaplin withholds nothing of himself when he acts, nor does he keep anything back. He plays the whole thing out right then. Compared to him, Woody Allen is miserly, a saver. He's in a series of numbers, in more or less successful scenes, in a whole series of very, very artful, very calculated gags, very local, very "spontaneous," and really very worked out. They are the "New-York-isms" of our time in the same way we speak of the "Parisianism." I didn't rediscover New York in *Annie Hall*, I found a life style, the way it is, the way I knew it in New York, rather sinister but not the perpetual Babylon-New York. And then love, in *Annie*

Hall, is only a pretext for gags, and this I am loath to accept. This is where Woody Allen's wretchedness lies, this worldly, constant recourse, this perpetual statement of self-mockery, of backbiting, of doing harm, of being mean. I hesitated . . . but it doesn't matter for me to talk this way about Woody Allen. In any case, he is lavishly praised by the critics, nothing can touch him anymore. Through his acting and his interviews, it's funny, I see that he must be impossible, that he must love nothing in life. In the end you can see everything with comic actors, in depth. In greater depth.

Chaplin's wandering has no geographical boundaries. Woody Allen's is limited to North America, N.Y., Manhattan. Chaplin lugs a Jewish European continent around with him. In other words, wherever he is, he's a stranger. Woody Allen is perfectly at ease in New York. In him I don't see that kind of unlimited, lost dimension typical of Jews—the towering Kazan—when they make movies. Woody Allen works in bits and pieces seamed together. I see the seams, whereas with Chaplin I see nothing. I see a straight line. I see a confident look that inundates the world. And then, in return, that sadness of Chaplin's. Yes, like that of a beast, of an animal trapped in a dependency from which he cannot escape. This animal has a fate that already anticipates and discourages all the interpretations we may give it, all the political levels.

JANUARY 5, 1980 NEWS UPDATE

It's good that these people from *Cahiers du Cinéma* let me talk about what I want. Today, January 5, 1980, on television, I saw Juquin and Marchais who were talking about the invasion of Afghanistan. So that's what you saw in their eyes, what you felt was coming, that hope for Soviet expansion. Unless it wasn't fear, but I don't think so, fear of not being up to their new billing. There was clearly until now a constant uneasiness, a double play, but now at last we've seen what that was covering up. They would be all smiles, talking about the freedom of peoples to self-determination. And now look. We've seen them twisted round, like mannequins. That's right. It took the invasion of Afghanistan to reveal their scurvy identity, of collaborators.

THERE'S NO MORE ANYTHING.
IT'S ALL STILL THERE
AND THERE'S NO MORE ANYTHING

There are no more streets where we can get together, it's crowded all over and no one is there, there are no more villages, there are developments, there are no more streets, there are thruways, the cities are blotted out on the ground, they go straight up, wall in the streets, there are no more openings on the sea, the city, the forest, there's no way out to escape, all the doors close on fear, political, atomic fear, fear of looting, of violence, of knives, of death, the fear of death decides life, the fear of food, of the road, of vacations, the fear of statesmen and scoundrels, the fear of the police like the fear of statesmen, the fear of statesmen like the fear of scoundrels, we don't know anymore where to go, where to put ourselves, one automobile takes the place of six to seven men, our automobile population is roughly three hundred million, it is increasing at the rate of the Indian population, a new absurdity sets in, it happens under our eyes, it is there, outside, on all sides, you could say that it isn't generated by man but by a divine power, so undecipherable is its presence; the borders don't change anymore, there are no more population movements, there are manpower movements, movements of Japanese but there isn't any more war, there are very few things, very, very, very few, the paltriness of present reality and of the convergence of self and the world is more and more palpable; sometimes, it's true, one changes, but it's quite rare, and besides we no longer know what we're changing, a washing machine, people no longer know what exists along with them, and this in their own country, they still have football, rock, movies, infinite expectation, they go to the movies in order to see fear confined to a film, for the most part they have lost the other side of their life, the so-called personal, solitary adventure, everything is upside down, you see old people reading comics in the midst of the drug scene, purse snatchers, financial religions, new philosophies, you no longer see love, you see the liberalization of mores, it's very, very annoying but it's probably necessary, who knows, you no longer see the passionate scenes of adultery we saw when we were young, those dramas, those tragedies, those tempests that would pass through lives and so on, that would knock down the house of cards, sweep it all away, now you look, nothing more like that, kindness all over, that's right, understanding, all over, and just think, look, oil, no more oil, the price is as high as champagne, champagne is as high as an automobile, let's not even mention a house, it's as high as the whole mess, so what can you do? It's all different and yet the whole thing is still there, all of it, you only need to look, but you understand, what's there is because it's all there, in the end there's no more anything whereas, like I was telling you, it's all still there, it was better before, it was in the other direction, more logical, there wasn't anything but it was all there since that's all there was.

3 8

GAS AND ELECTRICITY

I think younger generations are so accustomed to the idea of power, of being subjected to power, that they think it's like this for everything else, that it's a part of the state of things which goes hand in hand with the history of mankind. That this is the way things are, that it will always be like this. Like the police, power, like power, the police, couples, tax laws, flu, compulsory vacations, the post office, gas and electricity. Soviet Russia the same as the P.C.F., for many among them would fill the space reserved for the horror of the moment so that it not remain empty. You know, I agree.

GOOD NEWS

I decided not to renew the assignment of the option for *Moderato Cantabile* to Promotion Artistique de Films, the film company that bought back the film. Wrote and telephoned. The rights are free, from now on, for those who may have my consent or that of my son, after my death. That's that. If I were younger, I would have rewritten *Moderato Cantabile* without a script, only the book. The script done with Gérard Jarlot was bad, phony, as was Peter Brook's production. Jarlot wrote in a very self-conscious way, everything on the surface of the page. The same as Peter Brook's production.

OVERNIGHT MOVIES

There are films that stay with you, others that vanish in the immediate hours right after you've seen them. That's how I know whether or not I've gone to the movies: what, the morning after, has become of the film I saw the night before. The way it looks the next day is what I've seen.

Sometimes films become clear two months later. The majority of films are lost. There are films that don't ever change for me, like *American Graffiti*, from the first time I saw it till now, a joy; cinema, the way you say music.

THE TV SET

So, more of the same. Every day, everywhere, it's on the rise. The television malady. The set is dirty. It's a household object now, an old pot, a kitchen sink, but old and dirty. We've been hearing them, seeing them, for a very long time. They come into your house, they show off for us. You turn on the set and there they are, you turn it off. You turn on this poor set once more and there's another one. You see their life-size heads, they stretch their necks, they look toward you, then you stand in front of them to block them, you turn it off. They give us the same presumptuous, profoundly conniving smile. They talk to us in the singular language that likewise presumes to be self-evident, with the same staggering force of conviction, the same postures, the same zoom, then they go off in another vein to speak to you about France, about the quality of life, about the Olympic

40

games, and *we* see they have a tooth missing, they have laryngitis or a cold, a Cardin outfit, clean fingernails, a chateau in Périgord. The lie, they're all in it, we see that they lie the way they breathe, every one of them, we see it, see it so much we don't see it anymore. They come there to lie. It's when they have to lie still more than usual that they order television to come look for them so they can show off. *We* know, we see the lie on television the way we see them, every one of them. There are the ones who are on the spot, and there are their commentators, their scavengers. Their phrasing in French is the same; sometimes we confuse them. What a gang. In general we tend to prefer the ones on late-night television, the ones who are on at four in the morning, because they're so tired. But what a strange effect they have on what they're talking about. Where they come from there aren't any more books, any more films, there's no one, no more news briefs. There's nothing but the show. It's mysterious. It's no longer a question of them alone but of the set, maybe, hard to believe that everything they approach they trivialize. And yet, as soon as they appear, a screen comes up between their image and we who are watching. As if the color were changing, as if the set were turning to gray, to the malady of gray.

Sometimes, you have to admit, what a joy, the great whales of Hawaii go by and chase them. Sometimes it's the baby seals, they are strange, they are painted different colors; the inspired youth of Canada discovered this, painting them in indelible color to make their fur unusable so as to save them from horrible slaughter.

L'HOMME ASSIS DANS LE COULOIR

I must have written this text, in its initial form, the year I wrote the *Hiroshima mon amour* screenplay. The words "You're killing me, you're good for me" are in this text for the first time. I wrote it for someone. I sold it ten years later to an English publisher for the sum of six hundred thousand old francs. It must have been translated and appeared without my name in London or in New York; I don't know, I never bothered to find out. I tried several times to write it again without any success. In this initial form, in fact, the natural setting for the house served only to accompany the facts; it was a Mediterranean setting that defined these facts but did not develop them. The house, the people too, remained in an isolation that had become unbearable for me. For a very long time I didn't know how to extend the scenes and especially how to *return* to them somewhere else, at a distance, in something else. And then in the period following the Aurélias, I discovered naturally how to do it. First I discovered the indefinite immensity of the landscape. Then love. Love was absent in the initial text. Then I discovered that the lovers were not isolated but seen, probably by me, and that this seeing was, had to be mentioned, integrated into the facts. And then that the orgasm had taken place, whereas it hadn't taken place in the initial form. Finally, *L'Homme assis dans le couloir* was completely rewritten apart from perhaps ten words which remained unchanged. I wanted to put the text here, in this issue of *Cahiers du Cinéma*, then some friends asked me not to do it, so I sent it to Jérôme Lindon.

THE MAN MADE WITH FEAR

When the farce is over we'll see the man manufactured with fear, the empty-headed man, the one from Kabul and from Prague. They've got him. The man who is frightened. He is afraid more than in China, more than in the virgin forest or on the stormy sea. This man is the most profitable soldier in the world. He is entirely at the mercy of the one who provokes his fear.

Why? we ask. Why want the whole man, the whole world? We don't understand. We don't see the *point*, what they would get out of the hegemony of Europe. We have the feeling of being in the presence of an invalid on tranquilizers. The tranquilizer, their valium, their sedative, being here the American continent, the fear of the U.S.A. This fear is different from the prevailing fear they achieve. It is the fear of not getting to rule the whole world bled white, reduced to the level of a Poland.

They're afraid of not being frightening enough. But here, facing this oceanic continent, they are incapable of making the fear they spread prevail. And in this case their fear, contrary to that of being killed, is of not being able to kill. In relation to the U.S.A., they are like Hitler Germany in relation to their country in 1941. But here they are not getting through at all. It's not a question of defeat but of an insurmountable geographical impossibility. They are therefore facing the earthly design of their pain, perhaps the only pain they suffer, which is that of not destroying.

But, and it seems they already feel it coming, the business of manufacturing fear is in the process of cracking, of being defeated. Their powerlessness in terms of geography is coupled now with a powerlessness in a new, inevitable sphere. It's the new look that Soviet Russia is taking on in the eyes of the people who are watching it. Despite their terrifying near-sightedness, the leaders, the dynasties, must all the same see that they're no longer facing the crowd, and that it will be more difficult than it was. In my opinion, they went to Kabul in order to stir up anew the old fear that they spread, to regroup it, but even there, the old fear did not respond in the way they were accustomed. The Afghan peasants dared to fire on Soviet bodies and behind them was the whole international freedom movement. In my opinion, they must begin to see the worst, namely that their only colony will remain the gulag. This doesn't mean that the end will be soon, it may last a hundred years; it means that nothing can begin in Soviet Russia anymore, that what is already there has already begun to end.

What is also new is that it isn't from the people who govern them that the people of the world have learned what Soviet Russia is, for those who govern all have an unspoken longing for this taming of the Soviet man. No, it's rather for and against these crooks that they've seen what was going on, and this from the beginning up to the present, namely that history had begun with the idea, the marvelous transparency of the idea in its infancy, before being put into practice, before the start-up of the machine. When the splendor of the man to come was one with the splendor of the idea. People know, everything started here, from this convergence, evil as a whole.

RENOIR. BRESSON. COCTEAU. TATI.

Renoir?

There's a movie I particularly like because it reminds me a lot of the outposts in the brush when I was a child. It's *Le Fleuve (The River)*. I don't like the girl who writes poems but I like that child who wants the snake. I like those slopes that look out over the Ganges, those verandas, the siestas, the gardens. I don't like the Indians who are in the film. Showing them is pointless. Nor do I like that kindness that pervades everything. Love is over-played in Renoir. *La Règle du jeu (The Rules of the Game)* illustrates this for me: desire replaced by its pavane. At best by its distortion—among the servants, right? I don't remember very well.

Bresson? Cocteau?

Bresson is a very great director, one of the greatest who has ever lived. *Pickpocket, Au hasard Balthazar (Balthazar)* all by themselves could stand for cinema in its entirety. Cocteau I scarcely know. I can't find words to talk about his work because I have never thought about it. I think Cocteau's work is very beautiful, but for others rather than me. Once these people start talking about film, I know they love Cocteau.

Tati?

I absolutely adore him. I think he's perhaps the greatest film-maker in the world. *Playtime* is gigantic, the greatest movie that has ever been done on modern times. It's within the scope of *A la recherche du temps perdu (Remembrance of Things Past)* and, within the scope of the city, this is the only time you can say: it's the people themselves who are performing. That's why I think the movie didn't succeed: "the people" is an abstraction, and this people loves more than anything else the story of the individual left to his fate.

However, with Tati, I feel on less familiar ground than in Bresson's films. Bresson moves me to pain. Tati to joy. But probably Tati wrings fewer things from me than Bresson, he's less wrenching. We ought to institute this kind of criticism: not to talk about film without a concern for things of this world but from the self relating to the film. When I see *The Night of the Hunter, Ordet, City Lights,* for the fifth time, it's as if I were renewed every time in the presence of these films, and at the same time amazed at being the same me through the years of my life.

Duras?

I don't like everything by Duras, but *India Song, Son nom de Venise dans Calcutta desert (Her Name of Venice in Calcutta Desert), Le Camion (The Truck),* and now *Aurélia Steiner,* I know are among the most important things that have been done in cinema for all time.

Godard?

He's one of the greatest. The greatest catalyst of world cinema.

Bergman?

No. I liked certain movies among his early ones, like *La Nuit* *des Forains (The Naked Night*)* but differently, no, I don't like him anymore, I don't like him. I see that I never liked him even when I thought I did. *Persona* and *Le Silence (The Silence)*, that's hot air. In the classroom teachers would say: Well written, but. . . . He's the image of the great filmmaker who aims for American audiences and a whole sector of French audiences that aspires to a cultural posture with regard to cinema and which wants to make us believe they love cinema the way they love literature, the "fine things," works of art. The pretense stops there, with Bergman. The Americans have never presented a retrospective of Dreyer's work. So they take Bergman for Dreyer and vice versa. You can't like both, Bergman and Dreyer, no, that is impossible.

* *Sawdust and Tinsel* in England.

RACINE, DIDEROT

We no longer know how artists spoke. Neither Racine. Nor Pascal. Neither Diderot. Nor Shakespeare. Nor Bach. The current principles of effective speaking in the theater make me run: "You must be quick, not lag, avoid pointless breaks, get straight to the point." The aim is that the "spectator not have time to get bored." He has so little time for this that he leaves the theater without really knowing what has transpired before his eyes. In *Ubu Roi*, directed by Peter Brook, not only was the text spoken very fast but poorly pronounced. Very few of Jarry's words could be heard. It was odd. Peter Brook was putting the performance ahead of the text which he must have considered to be secondary, a little schoolboy ringleader. To stage Jarry and do it in such a way that one can't hear! Imagine this with Bérénice, for example, and yet that's what happened, you heard only a tenth of it.

THE CRITICS

I have the feeling that the established movie critics don't bother anymore except with movies that cost a lot. Even if they say a movie isn't very good, if it has a big budget they say it in three columns. We know that the movie cost a lot by the length of the articles.

I think it's true that critics today function like relays of PR people, that they are completely dependent on the work of the PR people.

Yes, for *Le Matin, Le Monde*—apart from Claire Devarrieux. Now even *Télérama*. Sole exception: *Libération*. From now on, when there are two pages on a movie, it's because the budget exceeds the billion mark. Very few critics came to see *Aurélia Steiner*. The budgets weren't big enough. I think it isn't conscious, they're going to be amazed to read this. But it's true; they don't put themselves out anymore for low-budget films. Maybe they'll see them on vacation.

It's basic. People are much more impressed by big bucks than before.

They're no longer the people who discover movies. Except Devarrieux and Cournot, who are truly free and see everything, the others no longer see movies for the pleasure of seeing them.

Maybe there is a critic's burnout. There are a lot of movies on one hand. And then there are a lot of critics who have once been disappointed by the so-called "avant garde," "marginal" cinema. I've seen that with Siclier; he is absolutely sincere.

It's true, if you want to have a good laugh, you can imagine three or four established reviewers at a press viewing of *Aurélia Steiner Vancouver*, which cost five million old francs. It's unthinkable. I don't hold a grudge against them, but they ought to double the size of their teams. As film critics, how can they bear not to see certain films which they are told are important? It's hard to understand. There are a few who are completely unknown to me, who are always there, faithfully, when I publish something, book or film. They try, but like militants, to defame what I do. I'm told their names and then I forget them. Not them. They come to see, they read, they don't forget. This has been going on for a very long time, years and years, These people act in general out of a hatred to be kept up, right?

Yes, it's a tradition.

To assert their personality, right? Because it would seem that no one could hate so persistently without having made up one's mind in advance, prior to reading, to seeing, right?

20 MAY 1968: DESCRIPTION OF THE BIRTH OF THE STUDENTS-WRITERS ACTION COMMITTEE

Only once are there sixty of us. It's the 20th of May at the Sorbonne, in a room of the Philosophy Library. The matter at hand is the Constituent Assembly of the Students-Writers Action Committee. Fifteen are famous: writers, journalists, television commentators. Forty others, not: writers, journalists, students, sociologists, sociologists.

Some resolutions pass by unanimous vote. A boycott of the ORTF* in particular.

There are numerous speeches. The ones most listened to are those of the television commentators. Most of the others are inaudible. Two presidents succeed each other. It proves useless to elect a third.

Several times it is proclaimed that "everyone must speak." In fact, six or seven manage to do so, including the television commentators and students. The students because they severely criticize the undesirable development of the Assembly. The commentators because they are talking about Television.

No matter. Projects are outlined, often in detail. Committees are appointed. An administration is set up. A headquarters will be guaranteed.

The good will gushes, imposing its good intentions.

The committees will never meet. Those who come forward in stunning spontaneity—to guarantee the headquarters and the administration—will return, some only very rarely, others never. No headquarters, no administration will be guaranteed.

Those who are the most voluble will be the least constant.

* Organisation de Radio et Télévision Française.

53

For the most part they will be seen only once, this one time. The next day, the first drain occurs.

Out of sixty, twenty-five return. Not a single television commentator. Some sociologists, still. Writers too, not as famous as the day before. Students, yes. For the journalists, it's over.

The language is not as lofty. The discourse digresses.

An average is set in the course of several days: fifteen to twenty come every evening to the meeting of the Students-Writers Committee. They are not always the same ones. Except for three or four.

These make up the resources of the Students-Writers Action Committee. Starting from their concrete incumbency, at the agreed place, at the agreed time, the Committee is constructed.

At the end of three days—the Committee then emigrates to Censier*—a second drain occurs. A certain number of writers, as a group, leave the Committee, take over the Literary Society and, behind closed doors, found the Literary Union which will take the writer firmly in hand, in the strictest sense of the word, and will at last ponder the writer's status, role, interests, and, still behind closed doors, the writer's wound: language.

This departure, the main one, separates writers from writers.

Although theoretical—out of about thirty, three or four would come to the Committee—this departure plunges certain Committee members into bewilderment for several hours. Except for the three or four and, soon, a few others.

For two weeks more, the same average as there was at the Sorbonne is set.

Around the three or four, who are now seven or eight, different comings and goings numerically keep the Committee going every evening.

---

* A branch of the University of Paris.

Two or three students come irregularly, as critics. Always very carefully listened to during this period. Then, less and less.

Sometimes someone comes whom we've never seen before, comes back eight days running, then never again.

Sometimes someone comes whom we've never seen before, and keeps coming back.

Sometimes someone comes whom we've never seen before— where does he think he's come?—reads the newspaper, and disappears forever.

Sometimes someone comes whom we've already seen, or seen again.

Sometimes someone comes whom we've never seen before, comes back a few days later, then at intervals less and less far apart, then, suddenly, stays.

Often it's a matter of a single visit. Someone comes, looks, sometimes listens, and disappears. Sometimes someone comes, offers a poem in manuscript or reads a poem. Takes off again for Switzerland. For Montreuil.

A month goes by. And already the absences are noticed: the Committee is set.

In general, the same reasons make some flee and others stay.

The main reason is the composition of the Committee. It is impervious to all analysis. Chance, at the intersections of streets, would accomplish almost the same thing. The newcomers, unable to label the "milieu" into which they've chanced and no more able to explain "why" these people are gathered together, flee.

The other reason—the effects of which are felt even sooner —is the very business of the Committee.

Every day, for several hours, with a relentlessness that could pass for lunacy, the Committee collectively develops texts. As a rule, the newcomer doesn't resist this more than twice.

Unconcerned with people leaving, the Committee, tirelessly, continues its text development.

55

Two out of three times, the newspapers neglect these texts or put them in belatedly, as filler. What does the Committee care. It goes on.

It's the hell of collective development that determines the daily selection—once Massa's gang is gone.

Endurance varies according to a mysterious criterion. Here one can therefore proceed only by empirical analysis. This is what can be said: not holding out against this hell are the writers who one might have thought—beforehand—wouldn't hold out. Holding out are those who one might have thought—beforehand—would hold out.

The difference in the beginning, between those who stay and those who flee quickly becomes a new difference, getting bigger all the time, between those who have stayed and those who have fled.

Those who stay and those who flee use the same word to name the senseless rehashing of the sessions as well as the uncommon endurance needed to hold out.

—It's IMPOSSIBLE, each group says.

To repudiate a text is also to develop that text.

Such a text which, if it were read somewhere else would bring agreement, is rejected here. The first impulse is to refuse, to refuse the text submitted for judgment. The training for approval is such that once freedom is given rein, the first thing it does is to REFUSE.

Naturally, it's the work of an INDIVIDUAL that is submitted to criticism and collective development. Otherwise, collective development is illusory. Still otherwise, meaningless.

At first reading: distrust is at its peak. Right away, the text is put on trial to bring out—again and always—the irreducible isolation of the thought process. Its author, unrecognized, is objectively punished precisely for his irresponsibility. The "fruit of his womb" is massacred.

At second reading: distrust yields. Third reading. Fifth reading. Behold, the INDIVIDUAL having served his sentence, the community gets down to work.

Put through the mill, tossed out, ridiculed, repudiated, GONE, a text comes back to life. And often in a form scarcely different from its initial one.

Thus, with just a grammatical change, this text becomes COMMUNAL. It has gone through the tunnel. Comes out. Takes wing.

—I'm bored here, a writer declares.

We don't see him again. But his leaving is embarrassing. Though predictable, his impatience redefines him in our eyes. We realize afterward, on reading what he has written, that in fact all he has done is to move safe and sound from the old to the new.

The texts coming out of the Students-Writers Committee are almost always models of precision. Yes. They bear no trace of the enormous difficulty of their birth.

This difficulty is experienced as the main attraction of the business of collective development. It defines collective development at its very core.

It is the effect of each one's resistance to the activity of the group. Of each one's bad faith in the face of the objectivity of the group. Of each one's subjectivity in the face of the objectivity of the group. It is as old as the world.

The difficulty of each one in SURVIVING is similar in kind to this general difficulty. Here each one's difficulty is something that is shared. It becomes the difficulty of each and every one to make their survival a communal affair.

The Committee is IMPOSSIBLE TO LIVE WITH. This is the way it is made. The galley has been scudding ahead for four months. We are in the engine room. Every kind of sabotage—at night—has been tried. To no effect.

Nothing holds us together but refusal. Delinquents of class society, but alive, unclassifiable but unbreakable, we refuse. We push our refusal to the point of refusing to be assimilated into the political groups that claim to refuse what we refuse. We refuse the refusal programmed by the institutions of the opposition. We refuse that our refusal, tied up and packaged, bear a trademark. And that its vital wellspring dry up, and that its course be turned back.

The Students-Writers Committee has no militant organizational or party policy. None would have been able to hold out.

If the request is made—and it regularly is—to clearly state *just once* the ideas of each individual, this request is always rejected by the majority. There follows the relief of having escaped some danger. We say that we refuse to be divided by theory, the poison of the clear idea. We don't go so far as to say what would seem to be the truth: what we have built in common is less the stock of ideas we have acquired than the distrust we have for them.

Our refusal also covers the refusal to be divided by idiosyncrasies.

From the first day, our wariness was founded not only on the score of ideas but on one's private life, on a reference to individuality. And that happened naturally. Only insult takes its inspiration from "information," from the private trait.

—You who have. You who are.

Only insult, the better to hit home, resorts to the regressive value of having something on someone.

As a rule, all the Committee members have the familiar instinct for keeping silent about their reasons for being there instead of somewhere else.

Furthermore, only a slow psychoanalytic exploration could probably clarify—and feebly—the ins and outs of these reasons. The common denominator—and this for all Action Committees—would be *unbridled refusal*, whether conscious or not.

Everyone, through constant effort, preserves the FUNDA-

MENTAL COMMON FOGGINESS in which the Committee is immersed.

Often we don't do anything. We say:

I shall point out to you that we're not doing anything.

Habit.

The problem is somewhere else.

It's precisely in these periods when nothing is going on that the Committee *exists* in the most incontestable way. Why would one be compelled to do something? And risk his secret coming to the surface of his life, *to exist*.

Every day we are caught in the personal paradox of being drawn back to this hellish assemblage AMONG A THOUSAND POSSIBLE ALTERNATIVES, like this very one we would have chosen.

This assemblage has the effect on each and every one of us of an ATTRACTIVE REPULSION. We are constantly poised between the movement of rejecting it and that of coming back to it. It offers and denies itself at the same time. Its form is in process.

What is it all about? Maybe about something else entirely? Maybe.

We are the anti-cell. Around us there are only others like us, other Action Committees. No orders. No suggested model, no militants. Or else we refuse. Or else we swallow the poison. We function. We connect. No authoritative language here, no "line." Here, we don't *classify* anyone from the beginning. Here, we have disorder.

Lacking suitable references, let's continue by analogy: the Committee has the inconsistency of dreams. It has the importance of dreams. Like the dream, it is striking. And it is an everyday affair.

One can dream of a love without an object. The bond that connects us is chance.

For anyone coming from the outside, the apparent absence of some sort of affinity among its members *already* makes it resemble a society, but *still* a particular kind of society: COMICAL, OF CRAZIES.

—You are crazy, repeatedly comes out of the mouth of people who observe us.

We do not respond.

—You show a political unrealism that is beyond all limits.

Again habit. Unreality is still the crime. We will have to wait a hundred years.

We have held out against the last barricades, against the elections, against the summer, against the students dispersing, against their coming back, against the closing of the faculties, against their reopening, against the violent quarrels, against the worst insults. For two months no one has deserted us.

These proofs seem to us sufficient. We are eternal.

We are the prehistory of the future. We are that effort. That precondition for the latter to become possible. We are at the beginning of the TRANSITION. We are that effort.

We must never have had a profoundly alienating social existence. Otherwise we would not have held out. The ones who fled—in a word as in a thousand—were already firmly ensconced in the system. They can always say the contrary. To no avail.

No one is ever satisfied with the way the sessions develop. As a rule it is said that problems of detail take too much time. But what kind of general problems ought to replace them is only rarely defined.

A remarkable consequence of our endurance begins to be felt. Every meeting becomes a prelude to the next one. In such a way that the newcomer has a hard time, presently, in following what we are saying, in understanding *what is happening* at the moment, and what is the *object* of our concerns. Our sessions, even spread out over time, no longer circumscribe our connection.

The connection extends beyond them. We become incomprehensible to those who haven't joined us in time. They get things wrong.

—It's deplorable, *you are wasting time*. This is just the moment when you have to sign the texts, use your names.

Habit. The inner work that is done here is not counted in the evaluation. We are progressing, together, toward a rigorous freedom.

Those who flee with no regrets leave us, let's admit it, *already* with no regrets, on our side.

This recruitment, starting with each one's intention to be interchangeable, this enhancement of depersonalization, seems to us to be the only revolutionary stance. It goes with the enhancement of the person separated from his persona.

We have decided, as a majority, to publish a bulletin that will, we hope, reflect the experience.

We don't know if the Committee will hold out against this test.

N.B.: *The above text was rejected by the Students-Writers Action Committee. It was judged too "personal," "literary," "malicious," "false." The breaking up of the Students-Writers Action Committee originated in this rejection. L'Observateur—several years ago—published a part of it as well as passages by Maurice Blanchot and by Dionys Mascolo that were also supposed to appear in the Bulletin of the Committee. Those two signatures alone were mentioned, mine was omitted.*

FOR JEAN-PIERRE CETON, GREEN EYES

Come, come let us be off together this springtime afternoon, come, let us go through the city, let us talk, of everything, it's the happiness of life, to watch the movement, the city through the shop windows, the yellow light, let's keep on going, let's keep on staying, there and there again, to watch the city behind the shop windows, the yellow light it sheds, let us talk, of leaving, of staying, of writing, of killing oneself, you see, come for nothing, to hear the sound, the sound of foreign languages, the cries, the din, the river, the sweetness we speak, look at those vultures gliding above the valleys, look, in search of their prey, the wars, you know, the camps, yes, listen, the trains, running through Europe, from hunger it's said, and the dead, again, yes, you know it, yes, everything is similar and nothing is, no nothing since we are there, us, yes, listen, listen to that emptiness that is coming, new, the new adventure, let us stay together till evening, let us watch our long shadows on the sidewalks, let's stay together up to the slanting light, the evening, let's watch the night come, the other side of life, that turning back, scarcely can it be seen, scarcely can it be felt, that sliding back, that supple pivot, and then here, here they come, the genies, the genies of darkness, light-footed, they come, listen, the new harvests, those of the non-workers, those who will do no work again, will not suffer, will discover their fitness in the unlimited leisure of life, look, listen, that strange time, it is coming, long, it is long, slow, there is no more work, there will be no more work, the long stretches of unemployment of the end of the twentieth century, you've heard, have begun, are going to stay, to become time honored, let's say the same thing about summer, the summer is beginning, let's say it like that, the summer is beginning, the long days of summer, they are slow and profound, will stay that way for eternity, come, the proliferation of jobs has ceased, the

63

proliferation of trouble too, it's also not worth the trouble any-more, they not lying anymore, no more work, no more workers, come let's talk, again, of everything, it's the happiness of life, of this ocean city, this is where the city will rise from the waters, from this river, she's the one from the other side, listen, look at her, she's coming, she's the one who is coming, her, the loss of the world, look, here she is, you recognize her, she is our sister, our twin, she's coming, greetings, we smile at her, so young is she, so beautiful, with her white skin, her green eyes.

CHAPLIN, YES

Yes, Chaplin. He had no capacity for reflection, no hypothet-ical turn of mind, no judgment. He always went off into com-edy; in other words, comedy never left him. That comedy was wedded to the real and reflected it back to him. That was the way he grasped it and saw it. He saw Nazism as an atrocious circus but as a circus, Hitler as a bloody fool, Landru as a laborer in crime. Chaplin saw nothing in itself. He conceived of hu-manity as a damnation in which he let himself go. He would float along, drift along.

Chaplin's greatness. All by himself, he was the crowd. Drowned as in a bottomless pit. Nothing would stop his fall. The event would drop to the deepest part of him. It would be lost and Chaplin would let it be lost, he would let go. When the event would come back to him, after some time in him, in forgetful-ness, especially in the unintelligible, it's then that Chaplin would recognize it and would make it concrete. Chaplin is not a whole person. He is an inspired cripple, a hiatus of the cinema. He is mentally impoverished. Mentally retarded.

It's said that Chaplin's greatest stroke of luck was to have arrived on the scene in the period of silent movies. I say that this dimension of the silent movies has never been reached in the talkies.

SOLITUDE

One finds people too alone in society today. To say it this way means nothing, I think. There are people who are impossible to live with whom everybody runs from precisely because they don't have a gift for solitude. People who do not see, do not hear, who fill up life at any price. Terrified people, isolated by their very terror at the idea of life's solitude. Their terror terrifies us in turn. If solitude is discussed, we think that people are at the same time too alone and not alone enough. Most people marry to get out of solitude. To live with, eat with, go to the movies with. Solitude is blurred but not defeated. The guarantee: recourse to the other who is always there. A lovers' couple is short-lived. It never survives marriage. The couple is Christian in all the Western societies, always. But the illusion remains intact, with every budding couple, that it will be the exception to the rule. To love, that's what it is. The couple. The end of the individual adventure whatever its nature—maternity, on the contrary, I see as a deliverance from oneself, I see that one doubles oneself through it with a child, that one grows through it with a child, that one does not share with him, the other. One cannot do anything from within the couple but to wait for that wonder, the days of love, to run out. The couple, for itself, is an end in itself. You don't make anything as a pair, nothing, not even a child, it is made alone, not even love, it is made somewhere else when it strikes; here, in the couple, you don't experience it anymore; you while away the time, a lifetime. You pass over life. Life skimmed over isn't wounding. Solitude is bearable that way; it's no longer isolation. It's on this score that the couple is enviable and that it seems like a brilliant formula for the passage of a lifetime in every society in the world. One is in a constant reference to a faithfulness that is framed as religious taboo. Our love was so strong that we cannot be unfaithful to it without blaspheming against God. Young people who say they haven't known, and do not know this torture, cannot be believed,

or else they're talking about something else, about getting set up together, about setting up house, but not about love or desire. This torturé, this ethic, affects every area of life. If I'm writing, I am failing someone. If I am loving "somewhere else," I am betraying the love of he or she who is waiting for me. If I am going off I am leaving, if I'm putting distance between us I already want to leave. Responsibilities nail one to the ground. Happiness doesn't work. Doesn't work with freedom. The ordeal of freedom is probably the hardest of all but it concerns another and terrible happiness. When one speaks of people alone, it's also there, in those couples who call themselves happy, stable, that the people alone are found. There are children. Work. They make love on Saturday afternoon. They no longer feel desire for one another but a deep affection. Every night they dream about a new love. About new desire. They say nothing about the dreams. The dream becomes guilty of betrayal. The betrayal is what remains the most genuine part of the love. Which allows for waiting.

The woman of Hiroshima is alone; she has been returned to solitude by the death of the young German. She remains alone in marriage, in maternity. Anne-Marie Stretter has a lover but for them, the main reason for the couple, the end of solitude, no longer exists. Despair here has free rein. Anne-Marie Stretter is in a permanent solitude. And when she dies, she dies alone. He will make no move to prevent her from killing herself. There is no greater solitude than that experienced by Aurélia Steiner. We can always talk about projects to come, about a movie to come, for example; that won't stop the movie, the project. Whereas a book that is in the process of being created is a space that cannot be violated or one pays the price of not having it exist. By exposing a book to other eyes you take away from it something of yourself, and for good. The book moves on and while it is moving on it is nothing but the potential existence of life, and

like life it needs all the constraints, of suffocation, of sorrow, of delay, of suffering, of every kind of hindrance, of silence and of night. It first has to go through the disgust at being born, the horror of growing up, of seeing the day. When it finally exists it will show no trace, nothing, of its initial journey. But while it's doing it, it must do it alone, without any help. One cannot prematurely decide in advance what it will be, display the mystery that governs its destiny without damaging what it is becoming and especially without making that mystery fly away forever, so that it is forever changed. You have to go through this journey with the book you are giving birth to, this hard labor, the whole time of its writing. One acquires a taste for this wonderful misery.

I am talking about the written text. I am also talking about the written text even when I seem to be speaking of cinema. I don't know how to talk about anything else. When I'm making movies, I'm writing, I'm writing about the image, about what it should represent, about my doubts concerning its nature. I'm writing about the meaning it ought to have. The choice of the image which is then made is a result of this writing. The writing of the film—for me—*is* cinema. As a rule, a script is done for an "afterwards." A text, no. Here, as far as I'm concerned, it's the opposite.

When I wrote *Aurélia Steiner Vancouver,* I wasn't sure I could film it afterwards. I wrote it in the happiness of not shooting it afterwards. I wrote it. If I had not been given five million to shoot it, I would have made a film noir, a dark videotape. My relationship with cinema is one of murder. I began to make movies in order to reach *the creative mastery which allows the destruction of the text.* Now it's the image that I want to affect, to diminish. I'm at the point of envisaging a master image, which could be indefinitely superimposed on a series of texts, an image that would have no meaning in itself, that would be neither beautiful nor ugly, which would take its meaning only from the text that passes over it. With the image of *Aurélia Steiner Vancouver* I'm already not very far from the ideal image, one that will be sufficiently neutral—let's be serious—to avoid the trouble of making a new one. People who make miles of pictures are naive and—have you noticed?— sometimes they come up with nothing. With the darkened film I would thus have reached the ideal image, the one that blatantly murders cinema. This is what I think I've lately discovered in my work.

If I don't remember the text the way it has suddenly appeared on the page, the written voice, I begin over again. I started *Night* over four times. With *Le Camion* and *Aurélia* I found the original path of the voice right away. You see, I'm not trying at all to develop the meaning of the text when I read it, no, not at all, nothing of the sort; what I'm looking for is the original state of this text, the way one tries to remember a distant event, not experienced but which one has "heard about." The meaning will come later, it doesn't need me. The voice of the reading on its own will give it without my intervening. The way it is read out loud is suggested in the same way that it was suggested for you alone, the first time, without a voice. This slowness, this lack of discipline in punctuating the text is as if I were undressing the words, one after another and I discover what was underneath, the isolated, unrecognizable word, stripped of any kinship, of any identity, abandoned. Sometimes it's the space for words to come that is being suggested. Sometimes nothing, barely a space, a form, but open, ready for the taking. But the whole thing must be read, the empty space too, I mean: the whole thing must be recovered. One notices when one speaks, when one listens, how easily words can crumble and turn to dust.

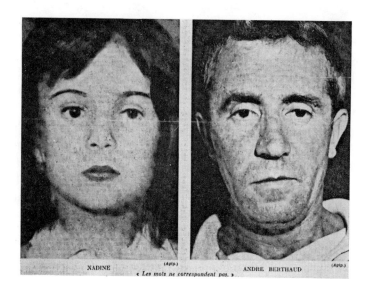

NADINE   *(Afp.)*   ANDRÉ BERTHAUD   *(Afp.)*
« *Les mots ne correspondent pas.* »

NADINE FROM ORANGE

The story of Nadine from Orange, kidnapped, then returned safe and sound by her abductor.

France-Observateur, 12 October 1961.

It was on the basis of the "interrogation" of André Berthaud which was aired on television that I went to see his wife. I waited an hour outside her door, she didn't want to let me in, she was trying to get me to go away, she was holed up in terror and horror. And then she opened the door. We talked a lot. While she was talking she was listening for sounds from the stairs, the police still—I remember the picture: the man in the police station on rue des Saussaies, flattened against the wall, in the light of the projectors, the policemen barking over the game after the kill, they were sharing him between them like a feast. You're going to say it, aren't you? Say it . . . say that you fondled her . . . dirty bastard. . . . Eighteen years later, the thing is still intolerable, still with us. He asked to go to the toilet and there he plunged a knife into his heart, he who didn't know anything, knew how to do it. I remember the effect of this news, that very evening, on television. People's anger and, suddenly, their refusal to be manipulated, their refusal to swallow the police's version according to which A. Berthaud had committed suicide precisely because he was guilty. Big upset for the police, this business.

Now, just like when the incident occurred, I see A. Berthaud's action as not being the only response he could have made but above all as a refusal, that's all, a refusal to respond, that is to start taking part in the deadly comedy of the police. His mental retardation, here, is an advantage: he will die the way he has decided—Yes, this evening, all of a sudden, nobody at the police station anymore, no more "work," they are alone, they have been "had," "tricked": the man is dead. The love between the man and the child will remain unpunished, death has put an end to it. I believe absolutely in this love. A. Berthaud and the little girl loved each other. The medical report was explicit: little Nadine had not been raped. Rape could have occurred. It did not occur. It is possible that there was a transfer of the unperpetrated rape in A. Berthaud's final act, probably—you don't see so violent a love without this consequence of desire— but for me that's the very reason why rape was transgressed: the strength of the love for the child.

Feeling that it's none of my business, that it's nobody's business. Rape did not occur.

I tell myself suddenly that it's rather strange that the murderers of four policemen in recent months were picked up in forty-eight hours and that the murderers of Pierre Goldman* still hadn't been picked up after three and a half months.

M. Duras: How did it begin?

Mme. Berthaud: *Nadine's cousins were friends of my daughter Danielle. That's how my husband and Nadine got to know each other. They all got together on vacation at Notre-Dame-des-Monts. It is thought that they knew each other for a long time, but that's wrong. Nadine and André only became acquainted during the last days of our vacation between August 31 and September 4. It was during those five days that they took a liking for one another.*

—What happened between September 4th and Tuesday, the 26th, when he left?

—*He returned to spend three days at Notre-Dame-des-Monts without us, to see Nadine again.*

—During the five days on vacation, while you were at Notre-Dame-des-Monts, what happened?

—*They were smitten with a crazy affection for each other. The newspapers didn't tell the whole truth. The little girl couldn't do without André either. Wherever we happened to be, she would turn up. They would play together, they would swim together. She would cling to his neck and go back into the ocean, like that, hanging on his neck. He would carry her on his shoulders. From the time she got up, she'd be looking for him. This seemed funny to us, and even annoying. Once, when she turned up at our place, he had gone off to go swimming three kilometers away. I had to get angry to prevent her from going the three kilometers on*

---

* Militant leftist writer, of Polish origin, jailed and sentenced to life imprisonment on murder charges, and then freed due to reasonable doubt. Goldman was an influential editor on the newspaper, *Libération*, and the review, *Les Temps Modernes*. He was murdered in 1979 at the age of thirty-five by three unknown men.

74

foot to catch up with him. Wherever we were, she would turn up. She would run away from her grandmother's place and would come to André. She would have liked to sleep, to eat at our house. Wherever we were, she would find us again. Once, when we'd had a picnic under the pines, she managed to find us. André was sleeping. We chased her away. And then André woke up. Then, of course, she stayed with us; he demanded it!

—How was André Berthaud with his children?

—*He loved all three of us in his way, loved us terribly. He would have killed anyone who touched his children. But I must say that never had he taken an interest in any child, never, the way he took an interest in Nadine, even in his own children. With Nadine, it happened suddenly. And he carried it to the utmost as soon as he saw her. You have to say that he was crazy. That he was a very violent man, a man of extremes, a very simple man. This experience between Nadine and him is that of a child of twelve who falls in love with a child of twelve. Never could I have imagined such a thing. When we left Notre-Dame-des-Monts, it was awful. She wanted to stay with him, he wanted to stay with her. Both of them were crying. They were desperate.*

—You were saying that he had gone off again to see her once more for a weekend? And that it was after that three-day weekend with Nadine that you began to worry.

—*Yes. He wanted to see Nadine again. He wouldn't stop repeating: "I want to see Nadine again." He didn't stop talking about the child. He wanted Nadine's photos everywhere, on the television set, on the mantelpiece, everywhere. We tried to take them away. And that's when he began to threaten us, to threaten our daughter Danielle. "If a single photo of Nadine is taken away," he'd say, "Danielle will never again see J." (J. is Danielle's fiancé.)*

—You think the fact that Danielle had gone with him to Orange . . . ?

75

—*Yes, I'm sure of it. I am sure he told her, "If you don't come with me, you'll never again see J."*

—Tell me more about that period preceding that decision to go off with Nadine.

—*He wanted to see Nadine again, see her again at any cost. He'd talk to me about it. "I want to see Nadine again. You don't need to be jealous of Nadine. I love her deeply. If she were fifteen or sixteen, I would understand your being jealous, but of Nadine, you don't need to be jealous." If I wasn't worried the first few days, it was because Nadine was nine hundred kilometers away from him.*

—What were you worried about at that time?

—*I was only afraid that he would go bother the little girl's parents, disturb them, in order to see her again, that he would get himself thrown out. Never was I afraid of anything else.*

—Was his passion for Nadine growing day by day?

—*Yes. We tried to cure him, the children and me. Nadine is a ravishing little girl. We'd tell him: "Nadine is dark skinned, she's losing her teeth, Nadine is ugly." He would get into terrible fits of anger. "There isn't anyone more beautiful than her," he'd say. Toward the end, in the final days before September 26, it was awful. He wasn't sleeping anymore. He wasn't eating anymore. He wasn't thinking about anything but the little girl. We would still try to make him smile, we would ask him to smile. He couldn't smile anymore. He couldn't do it. "If I saw Nadine," he'd say, "it would be better, if I saw Nadine, I would get well."*

—At that moment, didn't anything else matter anymore for him?

—*No, nothing. He was no longer concerned about us. But even when we returned from Notre-Dame-des-Monts, nothing mattered anymore for him. Like, you see, his son Claude who is twelve, he wanted to make him a champion cyclist. He'd bought him fantastic equipment. Every Sunday, for years, he'd go coach him in the Bois de Vincennes. He'd do it passionately. And after*

76

his meeting Nadine, he never did it anymore, never. This was painful for Claude. I remember: at Notre-Dame-des-Monts, Claude would chase Nadine away and sometimes he would even hit her to drive her away, he was jealous, and it's quite natural. But, just think, the little girl would always stay and André would always be looking for her again. Nothing could separate them.

—At that time, on vacation, weren't you worried?

—*No, not at that time, not yet. It was extremely tiresome, exasperating, to see them together all the time, not paying attention to anyone else, but that's all. It was after our return, especially after the weekend that things—an overwhelming passion he couldn't fight—got too much for André. And then I was frightened.*

—And you never had any doubt about the nature of this passion of André Berthaud for Nadine?

—*Never. People have bad thoughts. They don't understand. The rape of children is a common occurrence, so they said it was the rape of a child. I, you see, though I have never seen such a thing, though I could not even have imagined it, I knew it was something else entirely.*

—What?

—*It's impossible to say. Words don't do it. Love, yes, but not only that of a man for a woman, not only that of a father for a child. Something else again. I don't know how to say it.*

—Were you never afraid for Nadine?

—*Never, never did I see the slightest sadism in the passion André had for Nadine. Never. When the inspectors came, I always reassured them, always, I always swore to them that André would never do the slightest harm to Nadine. Even if I had never seen such a thing, this passion that Nadine and André had for one another, I knew that it would never have crossed my husband's mind to do whatever kind of harm to the little girl, never, never.*

You understand, he was a bit simple-minded, a very good man

—he would have given the shirt off his back—but just because he was so simple-minded, he was a little rejected by the neighbors, by the family, by friends. And when he met the little girl, he was overcome by the fact that she was so tender with him, that she sought him out all the time, that she was so sweet. She would kiss him like her father. Hanging on his neck, I tell you, the whole day. She was a child, the way I see it, who had never had the "advantages" of having a father. Her father is a military pilot and she almost never sees him. On her side too, it's extraordinary. It seemed odd to me, this story, at the beginning: now I explain it a little to myself. Maybe they needed each other. They were overcome. They had never delighted anyone the way they delighted each other.

—What was André Berthaud's nature?

—*Very simple-minded, I tell you, a twelve-year-old child. Very good. A child of divorced parents raised by his grandmother. Very unyielding. He would fly into fits of extraordinary rage, so extraordinary that if the inspectors had come to tell me that he had killed in the course of a quarrel, I wouldn't have been astonished. But Nadine, never, never would he have done her the slightest harm. What he loved most was sports, the outdoors. A man who never smoked, never drank alcohol, never anything but milk. Every Sunday, we would go into the forest of Senart or to the Bois de Vincennes. He was a man, you see, who would pick flowers. I was too lazy to bend over, not him. You see how he was, without ever getting tired of it, he'd be picking flowers.*

—In that same forest of Senart where he took Nadine?

—*Yes, you see I have my own idea about what they did in that forest. He must have been picking flowers for her, telling her stories, those stories for very young children. He loved those stories.*

—After he got back from Notre-Dame-des-Monts, did he write to Nadine?

78

—*I think so. Yes. He wrote Nadine some letters. I've never seen them.*

—Did you have conversations with him about suicide?

—*Of course, like everyone. He hadn't ever understood suicide. He'd say that to commit suicide it took an extraordinary courage he did not understand.*

—I have friends who watched television that night, who saw how he was insulted and treated by the "people."

—*I didn't see it. I was told that he was up against the wall, in the light of the cameras and that they were shouting in his face: "So, say it, you fondled her, dirty bastard!" and that everyone was insulting him and that he said nothing, that he had an awful look, awful. I think he killed himself because he was told he was a criminal, that he had fondled Nadine, whereas never, never, would it have crossed his mind to fondle Nadine, never, I can swear it, and that he didn't know that people, with their bad thoughts, could accuse him of this without any proof, and even give him the idea. He went crazy. I would like to do something. I would like to bring an action against the people who drove him to commit that abominable act. Do you think it's possible?*

—I don't think so. I advise you, however, to try.

—*I would like you to talk about my little Danielle who is in jail in the Vaucluse. I have received letters from her directors and from her colleagues in the house where she works. They all agree in saying that Danielle was a lovely friend, completely serious, and that they are ready to do anything to get her out of there. She was a child, Danielle was. Besides, she loved her father very much. And she was afraid for him, that he might go crazy, she was afraid for herself that her father would prevent her from seeing J., this young man she loves.*

—Was André Berthaud strict with his daughter?

—*Very. She was a little girl of eighteen and a half who'd never gone to a dance. Not once. He didn't want her to. He wanted her*

79

the way she is, serious. To tell the truth, she was afraid. And she wanted to please her father. She *didn't see any harm, either, in going to get Nadine because of the way she'd been brought up; she is still like a little girl. She had already gone with her father on moving jobs, once in Champagne, another time in the suburbs. I wasn't worried. André had never been very affectionate with his daughter. With his son, Claude, yes, but with Danielle, no. She wanted to be nice with this father.*

—What do you think would have happened if André Berthaud hadn't seen Nadine again?

—*I don't know. Maybe, in the long run, he would have forgotten her. But I'm not sure about it. I don't know.*

—If "people" hadn't forced him to commit suicide, he would have had to do barely six months' time, you know?

—*I know. People tell me. But what to do?*

80

A DIFFERENT CINEMA

Here the film says nothing. Its evolution is difficult to grasp,
it appears not to change, not to progress, not to go forward, to
move only in relation to itself, to a fixed point which it would
seem to have imposed on itself throughout. Change, apparent or
real, is not external to the film; the film contains it. So this
immobility, this fixed point around which it unfolds, holds it
within itself, closes it upon itself. Nothing gets away, nothing to
lighten its density.

I'm thinking right now of *Codex* by Stuart Pound,* with a
musical score by Phil Glass. The film is without a past, without
a becoming. The film beats time with the regularity of a metro-
nome. That's all it is, regularity and presence. The movement
of the film you can say is that of Phil Glass' music. Similarly,
you can say that the subject of the film is the movement instilled
in and imparted to Stuart Pound's film by Phil Glass' music.
Even if from time to time we stop briefly on shots of a woman's

* Winner of the Grand Prix at the festival of Hyères, 1979.

81

face, on open doors, on sets, these shots are integrated into the flood of music, they go forward with it, becoming part of its flow. You can also say that here is a pure cinema of intelligence, that here this intelligence is that of the simultaneity of sound and image. Simply this, intelligence of this, but of an intoxicating kind.

The film doesn't unfold, it acts. Very quickly an agreement is reached between the film and you; you go over to the other side, on its shore, meaning that while its axis stays the same, its range overtakes you and *you* go into it in turn. Even so, the film stays in its orbit, chained to its steel axis, that of its writing. Besides that, besides Stuart Pound's experiment, all is digression, loss of substance, loss of music, of energy and of space. When the distance is spanned between you and the film, you in turn are chained to the spiral, to the movement of immobility. Similarly, this movement acts on you, drawing you into its wavelength, its irresistible and immobile advance.

Hyères, Digne, the only places beyond money, the only places for cinema's passion.

"THE PENETRATION OF THE BODY OF AURÉLIA STEINER"

"I tell her: I'm going to give you a name.
You are going to utter it.
You will not understand why and yet I'm
asking you to do it, to repeat it without
understanding why, as if there were
something to understand.
I tell her the name: Aurélia Steiner."

*Isi Beller says that the sex act here is like a kind of metaphor
for what should happen when someone is called by name, when
someone is named.*

The black-haired sailor's penetration of the body of Aurélia is

*the name Aurélia Steiner which is written into Aurélia's body,
and Isi Beller sees Aurélia as the purveyor of this metaphor. In
other words, an inscribing and a wearing away, and again an
inscribing and a wearing away. She cannot seize this name, she
cannot seize this imaginary thing she creates for herself, she can
pin it down only by the penetration of her body, as if the name
were written there, in this body.*

*She is caught, he says, in a kind of coming and going between
the inscribing and the wearing away of the name and that's it,
the racial, Jewish orgasm of Aurélia Steiner—these are Isi Beller's
words. He also says that to fix the Jewish past, at this point,
would be to repeat what happened for the Aurélia Steiner born in
Auschwitz—the one who is described by the other eighteen-year-
old Aurélia Steiner, to repeat what happened for her at the time
of her birth, in other words the death of the two lovers killed by
her—the mother's hemorrhage after giving birth and the father's
hanging after stealing the soup for her, the child. This scene of a
double death she would experience in her orgasm with strangers,
that is, in a form of anonymous prostitution—the anonymity of
the crematoria, of the camps. I was convinced, amazed by the
hypothesis of the name being implanted in Aurélia Steiner's body,
but when Isi Beller broadens it to go back to the first experience
of this fixing [of the name], I am less convinced. It's a mysterious
scene, very difficult to elucidate and at the same time it seems
completely necessary. I believe in a more general, historical memory; I think that Aurélia Steiner, the child, would know everything in detail about her birth, that she could just as well have
seized upon another atrocity at random; any atrocity whatever,
suddenly visited upon the Jews of the white rectangle of Auschwitz.*

JUDEN

For me, it's not an insult when the black-haired sailor switches from the name Aurélia Steiner to the name Juden; he's letting himself be taken in, swept away by the strength of the curse that prevails over the race and the body of Aurélia Steiner; he isn't aware that he's no longer naming her but that he's calling her by the word that invokes her race and doing so, he enters into the vertigo of wild desire. This word becomes a word that takes him way beyond the limits of himself, an insane word, like those cried out in insane desire. This word fits Aurélia Steiner perfectly, her sexual pleasure comes with this word through which she completely rejoins the lovers of the white rectangle of death.

In your work there are always characters with a name and characters without a name. For example, the beggar woman of Savannakhet.

Here, it's a question of the name disappearing. Like the maiden name of Anne-Marie Stretter [in *India Song*], Guardi, wiped out on the tombstone. The beggar woman no longer needs a name. She has not forgotten the language, she has forgotten the children, she has not forgotten her birthplace, Battambang, but she has forgotten her name. There are still people who know the name Guardi, the name Venice. But the beggar woman's name, nobody in the world remembers anymore.

85

A DREAM

Eden Cinéma* *was having a run at the théâtre d'Orsay. And one night, after the performances were over, I dreamed I was going through a house with colonnades, that there were something like deep, interior verandas that looked out over gardens. On entering this house, I heard the tunes of Carlos d'Alessio,†—the waltz from* Eden Cinéma, *and I said to myself: imagine that, Carlos is here, playing. And I called him. No one answered. And my mother came out of the place where the music was coming from. Death had already taken her, she was already rotting, her face was full of holes, already greenish. She was smiling very slightly. She said to me: "I was the one who was playing." I said to her: "But how is that possible? You were dead." She told me: "I made you believe that to permit you to write* all this."

* Play, produced 1977.
† Carlos d'Alessio played the music for *India Song*.

86

THE DARK

Isi Beller was struck when I spoke to him about the film without pictures, about a dark film, about a film where a voice is reading a text. He says it's a basic element in a general approach to the explanation of my films: the dark. That there is not, of course, any redundancy between the text and the image in my films, that he sees a darkness inserted between the text and the image. He sees this darkness as the vehicle of a non-thought, a stage in which thought may topple, may be obliterated. He sees that this obliteration may meet the dark of orgasm, the death in orgasm. And that what happens for the viewer is that something in him opens up and causes him not to have to make that effort to put it all together which he does when seeing a commercial film, that is, to make the image and the word coincide. Here in my films, he isn't deciphering, he is allowing himself to be acted upon, and this opening up in him gives way to something new in the link that connects him to the film, this something being a kind of desire. According to Isi Beller, it seems to be the explicit and the implicit that meet in this interval of darkness.

You were saying: "In reading, we rediscover ourselves, and in going to the movies, we lose ourselves." And when we go to see your films, we do not lose ourselves. It is in the dark that we rediscover ourselves.

Yes, this darkness would perhaps be, in fact, a space for deciphering which would allow you to let yourself be acted upon by this film more than by other films. Here, you yourself must create within you the space for receiving the film, without being aware of it of course. In *Aurélia Steiner Vancouver*, when the sound fades, and someone is talking about the dim light, about the eyes, the hair, about the body in the mirror, when someone speaks of a veiled image and the beauty it reveals, this against the darkness of the great granite blocks where one can hurt oneself, tear oneself, I am not only at the movies but suddenly somewhere else, somewhere else again, in the undifferentiated zone of myself where I recognize without ever having seen, where I know without understanding. Here, everything connects, merges: the wound, the icy cutting-edge of the dark stone and the mild softness of the threatened image. The happy coincidence between word and image satisfies me here with evidence, with sensual pleasure.

THE NIGHT OF THE HUNTER

I always forget the beginning of the movie. I forget that the real father has been killed. I confuse the murderer of the father with the father. I am not alone in this respect. Many people have told me they've made the same error, as if this father were real only from the moment he was killed and that he is more involved in the life of the man who has inflicted this death than in his own. In *The Night of the Hunter* it's not life I see created, it is death. I do not see the father before he is dignified by the murder perpetrated on his person. I've seen the movie four times and I always make this error. I do not manage to see the father alive. After he has been killed, I see the criminal in his place. His place filled by the murderer. I've always seen and constructed Charles Laughton's movie on the basis of this error.

I see the mother affected by the same inexistence as the father, and, like him, killed. But there I see her killed by him through childbearing and drudgery, through poverty. I see her as not existing. The beginning of the movie I see as rigged and that Charles Laughton didn't dare to make a direct connection between the father as the criminal and his children. I do it for him instead. I say: the criminal is the father, and it's out of this butchery, out of this massacre that I see the children born and emerging as from a body and leaving it as one would a native land. Here, some day, the separation will be completed. What takes twenty years will take three years: the separation from the mother.

The children are small and nature is immense. They go down the highways, then a river. Highways between the rice paddies, embankments, slopes. They go down the Nile, the Mekong. They travel through deserts, straight roads between the deserts. They go down all of them. The criminal father with his horse

89

and his weapon, the naked little children, denuded by childhood itself. Around them, the southern part of a continent, of a country whose name we do not know. Everything is flat, lagoon-like, easy to cross. You see clearly in front of you but what's ahead is limitless. It's a relentless, regular development. Pursued by the criminal, the children can only always push further ahead. The criminal's solicitude is matched only by the flatness of the place. Continuous, never ending. It could last for twenty years, without any change in the evenness of his steps. The criminal wants the children's money which is stashed inside the little girl's rag doll and he calls the children by whistling a Negro spiritual ("Moses") that invokes the compassion of God. Depending on the distance that separates them, "Moses" will tell the children how far they are from death. The song will be the signal either of a respite, if he is far off, or of flight, when he comes closer. I approach the movie after the pursuit by the criminal, when the chase has ended, you could say. The children's small boat has run aground on the riverbank. They are sleeping. And as always in the movies, an old woman passes by, an old woman who customarily is in charge of charity, of sheltering cats, lost children. She will likewise shelter these persecuted children. We breathe at last, we are relieved about their fate. And then, that's when, for me, *The Night of the Hunter*, the real movie, begins. It lasts ten minutes. It attains a fullness which the American cinema has never reached as far as I'm concerned.

One comment before getting to this movie within the movie. I notice that all the people in *The Night of the Hunter*, children, parents, murderer, old woman, are perfect prototypes of the American cinematic bestiary. Which does its recruiting according to the grid of the social milieu. Real people are not to be seen in the movie, as in almost all American movies. These people fill the office of their roles as delegates from their social milieu. I tell myself that it's perhaps when it reaches this essential insipidness that the American cinematic product is at the height of its efficiency: product of contemporary consumption. No author. An absolute guarantee that nothing unexpected can turn up here. The expectation here being that the criminal father will be arrested and punished and that the children will be saved.

And now the movie within the movie unexpectedly takes place, the second *The Night of the Hunter*. Kind of a merging. That night, at the end of the chase, these people assemble. The old woman, both good and stern, crazy and effective, those innocent little children, that enduring notion of impunity. And that child-killer father, that devourer of sweet flesh, that swine hollow as an empty bag. Here they are all together in the scene of the merging, that place glimpsed between the old woman's house, the garden surrounding it, and the road going by. It's at this point in the movie that we have what I could call the miracle of *The Night of the Hunter*. What is suddenly established among these people is a connection which up to then is impossible to predict and which escapes all classification, all analysis. First it's a question of a way of behaving that the old woman invents and the criminal then repeats. These people, so different, suddenly agree to take the film in hand and decide its fate, as if an author were finally getting into the act and, liberating the movie, carrying it off, free. Suddenly, we don't know anymore what we are seeing, what we have seen. So accustomed are we to seeing in the same way. Suddenly there's *a switch*. All the narrative elements of the movie appear to have put us on the wrong track. Where are we? Where is the good, the bad? Where is the crime? The movie progresses with no morality. It ceases to be the classic fiction of fifty years of American cinema. It has no predetermined outcome, we have no indication of the way it's going to go. We no longer know what we're supposed to think of what we are seeing: the children clustered around the old woman —a touching, sacrosanct bunch—indistinct from one another, locked up with the woman. Similarly, there's the money locked in the little girl's rag doll. These successive forms of confinement are very visible. The bunch of children inside a solid house but one with wide openings through which one can see and through which one may be seen. Through which one sees the criminal and through which the criminal sees the clustered children and the old woman joined together. Through which we see that the old woman has no strength of a physical kind to combat the crime. That the killer-father, charming, handsome, laughing, planted on his black horse, athletically endowed, so young, is the very figure of evil. We see that if he were to get in, he would massacre old woman and children with a smile, that nothing could stop him from it, and that nothing in him, afterwards, would be changed by it. The father, unreal by dint of malefic-ence while already touched by death, by the malady of death. By this death that he wants to inflict and which is already overtaking *him*. In the space of the merging, that night, the murder would seem to enjoy an ultimate achievement: a curse would be revived from the history of mankind, from which nothing would yet have been erased. For the children, one could say that from then on, until the end of time, the criminal would be held out as a sort of deity of evil, of an essentially loathsome kind, so that no one could ever again approach him, upon whom no one could ever again look.

The murderers of Pierre Goldman: affected by the same malady of death. They are dead and don't know it. They are living dead and are unaware of it. Deprived of life. It makes one think of spoiled harvests, it makes one think of killing, of inflicting death in return. Those youths, in their basketball sneakers, supple and speedy runners, dead bodies. For a million old francs, have killed Pierre Goldman. For a million or ten million old francs, have killed. Didn't know who. They don't deserve to live.

So there he is, the movie criminal, handsome and laughing,

on his black horse, looking at the exposed bodies of the children, behind the openings in the house, like someone who is hungry and is watching the food, who is cold and is watching the fire. There's still the picturesque rifle belonging to the old woman, but it's there like a prop, a scarecrow, to no purpose. Given that the old woman is classed with goodness and love in the American myth, she cannot kill. So she improvises. The old woman therefore contrives to sing in order to get through the hours during which the threat of death exists, this passing of the night. A propitious night for murder, which slips away like the river. The old woman improvises by singing "Moses." She contrives to sing the very song that the criminal was whistling, calling on God for his help. Outside the house, and inside, between the criminal and the innocence of the children, the old woman contrives to raise this barrier of song. There's the miracle. As the song develops, the criminal goes through a transformation. A kind of grace, in turn—this grace being the commonplace of the old woman and children—overtakes him, welling up in him, wending through his wickedness, through his death, let's say the way childhood runs through life, and suddenly, his desire to kill appears naive in comparison with childhood, that immensity. Suddenly his crime appears to be the product of a whim, of an insatiable greed, of a child's willfulness. The old woman keeps on repeating her own song, which she sends back to him in the night through the intolerable evil he stands for. This song he now in turn begins to sing with the old woman. Sending it back to her in turn. The old woman's song has opened up childhood, the sluicegates of the infinite. Childhood was hidden, masked by crime. But who would have thought it? It was still there too, in the false father, as it is elsewhere, everywhere, whole; in the old woman, in the children, alike. And see how they come together. The criminal is singing with the old woman, they are singing together, loud and high like in church. Together. Both of them

93

know the song, the children likewise. I see that he doesn't know he's singing. He is singing. He hears singing and he joins in the song. You see people running and you join in the race. He's singing like before. Before what? Perhaps before the beginning of the world which the song relates. The old woman sings for him. First, she sings to make him understand that she is there, to keep him at a distance, to tell him that she is there, vigilant, to guard the children. And then afterwards her singing goes beyond this, to make the crime move away from the children's space, so it will be distracted, forgetting to kill, and relieving the criminal for a moment of the weight of his insanity. So that he will leave it alone for the time of a night. Then her singing goes even further than this. First her song is offered as a challenge, then it is shared by the father and then again, yes, it becomes a song of joy, of celebration. The criminal and the old woman together sing of the return to life, the father's last celebration, and the children are immersed in this song till morning. They sing at the top of their lungs. You can hear the song from everywhere. No one sleeps around the singing. The father still doesn't know he's singing, he will never know. During the course of the night, the song becomes an insurmountable barrier for the crime. With daybreak, when the singing stops, the contingency of the crime like that of work, of misfortune, of blinding reality, will return. The end of *The Night of the Hunter* is indeed a celebration, while the criminal himself collaborates in his own deliverance from evil, from that evil which is there in him like anywhere else, in this man like anywhere else, like Pierre Goldman's killers in their basketball sneakers. The criminal doesn't know how to be delivered; it's the others around him, the children and the old woman, who know. The criminal does not perceive his own life.

It's at the end of this night that the children recover their father in this criminal, that they recover their love. In one night. They have heard him loudly singing, forgetting everything, like

94

them. It's as if they had underrated him until then, as if they had not known the share of the father's irresponsibility and that up to then they had cast him in his sole role of criminal. This is the night of the criminal's reunion with his victims, night of the father who at the same time he created life created death. I think the confusion between the true father and the false father comes from here. At the end of this initiatory night, the children will be instructed in the mystery of evil and at the same time in its infinite relativity. At the end of the night too, this evil is vented by the father; leaving him it is going to catch up with and invade other people, those policemen who are going to arrest him. This handing over of their killer to those who will kill their killer which the children see—the children see their father arrested— is decisive. This father is going to die because of them. He is going to die for having wanted so very much to kill them. They are the cause of his death. The revelation is overwhelming. Like knowledge itself. One thinks of Moses, who so long as he was possessed by the idea of God, was unable to speak, was able only to cry out. The children cry out and give themselves up body and soul to the father, to their killer. With all the violence in them, they run away from the old woman and give themselves to the father. Overwhelmed by knowing, by love, the children run toward their father, offer themselves to him, tear open the rag doll, offer him their bodies, this money he has been coveting for so long, this reason for wanting so much to kill. No, the children do not betray the mother by giving away the money she had put in their hands for their survival. Here everything becomes confused and opposite to what one expects, the whole moral code leaving off. The children's action no longer falls within any analysis; it is impossible to circumscribe, nothing holds it back, there's no way to judge this major folly which is the children's love.

The movie ends with the real father being arrested before he has picked up the money. The children are safe. Evil is punished. But probably too late. The audiences in Portland, Salt Lake City, Oregon, Chicago, Paris, Berlin, were put off track by this ending and they contributed to the movie's not being a success.

It's strange, I see the end of *The Night of the Hunter* the way I see the end of *Ordet*. When, with the coming of daylight or the approaching night, the madman arrives with the child and speaks to him of eternity, I hear the song in *The Night of the Hunter*. The transformation of the two movies is developed in a similiar kind of merging, a similar kind of spread-out time span that is indescribable. Within the silence of the house, the madman and the child are joyful; they are denying death. When they cross the main room of the house, you hear the very loud, declaiming voice of the madman, so shrill, which mingles with the child's springlike, bubbling laughter, with his warbling cries. These noises, these bursts of chatter within the organlike rumble of the house's silence after the mother's death take me to the mingling of songs in the first light of day in *The Night of the Hunter*. They are cries that cannot be cried out, howls, songs, that cannot be howled, cannot be sung.

96

BOOK AND FILM
(*New Statesman*, January 1973)

One evening, in Le Havre—it was before the war—two women were in a neighborhood movie house for a show. At that time, a show included newsreels and a film. Had these two women ever gone to the movies prior to that evening? Or had they always gone "that way"? This, the person who saw the whole thing did not know. The fact is that these women who did not know that *newsreels* existed, that evening saw a movie in which the first episode took place before the intermission. Were they disappointed by their evening? Not at all. The witness (seated behind them) relates that after a certain wavering, punctuated by various hypotheses and reasoning, they had perfectly managed to integrate the newsreels into the story of the film. It didn't take them very long. Rather quickly, they had decided the content of the film, of *their* film. In this film, among other unexpected twists in the plot, the characters were attending a football game—why not?—and while they were at the game, the head of the government was inaugurating, somewhere else, a bridge, *while* still somewhere else, an earthquake was taking place, etc. After being watered down in an everyday, familiar set of circumstances, the main narrative again went on its way until the end of the show.

Certainly those kinds of viewers—with such a degree of creativity—don't exist anymore. The syntax of films no longer has to be learned. A child of seven knows how to read a film by the way it is put together. But even so, it's from the viewer's seat that the film is made. A book assumes an *approach* to it, not a film. A film viewer needs only *practice*.

Therein lies the essential difference between cinema and everything else. In this number [of viewers]—the largest—hence the most primitive.

You leave the house one morning, the sky is blue, it's sunny. You get this shock from the blue sky and the sun as soon as you've crossed the threshold. Somewhere in you, in your physical or mental constitution, the thing is expressed in the flash of sensation by: "Blue the sky this morning, sun." Later, when this lightning flash is recovered through time, if you want to polish it off, to tell it to someone else, you will *express* it in a sentence, oral as well as written, which will clearly state in what circumstances, one beautiful morning, in going out, you were struck by the blue sky, the sun. This will be, doubtless, the most common fate of the event you have experienced. But there are others, thousands, one of them, the poem, for example, or the cinema.

Of all the modes of communicating, cinema will probably be the last because it is presented as the most inaccessible—by virtue of the technique—and the most *separate* from the event. Actually, on the contrary, it's this means that will be the most apt to recreate the shock of the event, as: "Blue the sky this morning, sun," and to transmit it to the greatest number of people. Four words, two images connected to one another by a silent, invisible syntax, very close to coinciding with the original sensation in what is unspoken. This greatest number of people, who are they? Where do they come from?

A filmmaker's work on a film—let's not even talk about how the technical equipment gets in the way and holds back this work —occurs at a different *point* from that of the writer considering a book. Before getting to the film, the filmmaker has to go through a book which will never be written but which has the value of a written work in terms of its place in the creative sequence. He moves across this book and ends up in the space of his *reading*, exactly the place of the viewer. Look closely at certain films: they are readable, the thread of the writing can be discerned. The stage of the eclipsed writing, conscious or not, is visible; its space, its passage can be seen. (We're not talking of course about commercial cinema made from cooking recipes, which takes place at the opposite ends of any writing.)

At this point of his creation, the filmmaker's place happens to be the opposite of that of the writer in relation to his book. Can we say that in cinema we write backwards? We can say something like this, it seems to me. It's precisely in the viewer's seat that the filmmaker *sees*, reads his film, whereas the writer stays with an obscurity that no reading can yet read, unintelligible even for the one who is going to approach it. It's subsequent to this obscurity that we find the filmmaker at work. To make movies when you have written books is to change place in relation to what is going to be created. I face a book to be written, I am behind a movie to be made. Why? Why does one feel the need to change place, to abandon the place which one kept to? Because to make a film is to go on to an act of destroying the creator of the book, in short, the writer. It is to cancel him out.

Whether he is the author of an "empty" book or of a book "crammed with meaning," the writer, in fact, will be destroyed by the film. The writer who is in every filmmaker and just the writer, period. And even so, he will have said what he wanted to say. The ruin that he will become will be the movie. What he has "said" will be that glossy material, the pathway of images.

Between someone who has never written and a writer there is less distance than between a writer and a filmmaker. The one who doesn't write and the filmmaker have not dipped into what I call the "internal shadow" which each of us carries within himself and which can get out, pour out, only through language. The writer has gone into it. He has gotten into the integrity of the "internal shadow"; the essential common silence, he has worked out the distillation of this silence. And any action which impedes this distillation, cinema, for example, makes the written word regress. It's not true that cinema communicates the written text as much as the written language. Cinema makes the word revert to its original silence. Once the word is destroyed by cinema, it no longer comes back anywhere, not in any writing. And with the filmmaker, it's the very bent of his destruction that will become a creative gain.

It's on this defeat of the written text that—for me—cinema is built. In this massacre lies its essential and decisive appeal. For this massacre is precisely the bridge that leads you to the very point of any reading. And still further; to the point of just experiencing, which any real existence in contemporary society supposes. This can be said in another way: that the almost universal preference of youth for film is a choice—conscious or intuitive—of a political kind. That wanting to make movies is precisely wanting to go straight to the point where it is experienced: the viewer's perspective. And this, while avoiding, while destroying the stage—always the privileged stage—of the written text.

Capitalism's phenomenal pimping of the cinema from its beginnings has shaped four to six generations of audiences and we find ourselves facing a HIMALAYA of pictures that undoubtedly make up the largest historical collection of stupidities in modern times. Parallel to the history of the proletariat, there's the history of this additional oppression; the oppression of its leisure manufactured by the same capitalist system that enslaves it—its Saturday movies. For decades, only capitalism had the means to make movies. Access to the movies was a class privilege. We don't mean to say by this that it isn't anymore; it is simply a little bit less. But you have only to see the anger of the commercial filmmakers facing "this little bit less" in order to understand how much it's true, how much they mean to be bosses of world-wide cinema. I once heard Henri Verneuil talking about *Cahiers du Cinéma*; he was seething with rage, whereas *Cahiers du Cinéma* is one hundred thousand times less read than the movies by the same Henri Verneuil are seen. And to want to make movies is also precisely to get out of the role of consumer of capitalist cinema; to remove oneself, wean oneself from that reflex consumption of what one could say is the blatant fulfillment of the hellish circle of consumption, just that. By doing so we are making an accusation. It could be said that all cinema along the same lines is making this accusation.

THE BOOK, THE FILM

This morning, I was forced to confront the end of *The Vice-Consul* with a text I wrote years ago; I was wondering if I had taken this text from the end of the book. I therefore reread a part of *The Vice-Consul*. The amazing thing is that I realized I'd forgotten the book. I forgot it because other films had passed over it, because I made the film *India Song*. I rediscovered the book in wonder and great emotion and during my reading, the [versions of] *India Song* went out of my mind.

Lol V. Stein has remained intact, locked away in the book, confined to it. With Aurélia Steiner Paris, the child of seven, the little girl who is part of the war and the black towers, I perhaps should not do a film either. Let her stay in the book, like an absolute and untranscribable statement. Hellish.

AURÉLIA AURÉLIA TWO

Aurélia. Child. My child. The dance at S Thala is gaping once again. Aurélia is watching it. Aurélia has come out of the butchered body of L.V.S.* —Aurélia has replaced me. Taken my place. It's done. Everything is deserted, the sands of S Thala, where lunatics stroll, the sea as well. The wide balcony of the S Thala casino, facing the sunset, is empty. You hear the very gentle plashing of the winter sea. Sometimes Aurélia goes by. She looks at the sands and the sea. Yes, those eyes are blue. And in the evening, they become a limpid, bottomless darkness. Her hair is black. She is singing, now she's singing the melodies from the S Thala dance, she sings them like Jewish chants. Yes, she goes by the beach on stormy days, she listens to the wind, the fantastic frenzy of the sea, all of her leaning toward the empty abyss of the land. Pain is familiar to her, to Aurélia, and so is joy. Look.

* Lol V. Stein.

Someone saw the film and said he thought Aurélia had really existed in a remote village and that what I'd done was to have managed to get hold of her writings to make them into movies. "You know, Aurélia Steiner exists, it's not your voice one hears but hers. You've made her whole, she lives separated from you. I am all alone to face Aurélia Steiner, and I shake." (Letter from Serge Legroux. I have not met him.)

AURÉLIA AURÉLIA THREE

It's true that she is separated from me and that she's the one who is speaking in the films. All I do is listen to her and convey her voice; with every word, at every moment, I am careful, really at every moment, to join her and keep behind her, careful to account only for her writing as it comes out of her, still with no shape, almost with no meaning.

Cinema, compared to Aurélia Steiner's phenomenal power, is nothing. The film Aurélia Steiner Vancouver *was impossible. It was made. The film is admirable because it doesn't even try to correct the impossibility. It goes along with this impossibility, it runs alongside it.*

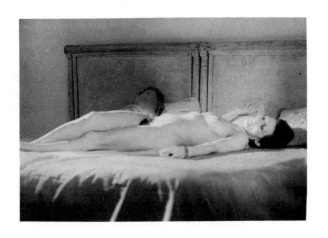

MAKING MOVIES, SEEING MOVIES

I think that one has the same reasons for making movies and for seeing them. I have close friends who don't go to see my movies, they go to see movies by others. They read all my books but they don't go to see all my movies. They don't see my reasons for making movies, they say it's not worthwhile. I, too, with every movie I make, find that it's not worthwhile. But one can also make movies that are not worthwhile making. Right now, instead of making movies, I am doing this issue of *Cahiers du Cinéma*.

AUGUST 25, 1979

On August 25, 1979, I find written in my calendar: "The sea is gray, black on the horizon, flat, heavy, with the density of iron. Immobile sailing ships. Welded to the iron sea. Silhouettes of beach strollers on this darkness of the horizon. Then, wind. In the afternoon, everything loosens up, turning to blue, starting to move again." It's a few days after I began Aurélia Steiner. *But after having sent someone the words about the sea written on a blue postcard.*

SCOUTING

Don't bother to go to Calcutta, to Melbourne, or to Vancouver, it's all in the Yvelines, in Neauphle. Everything is everywhere. Everything is in Trouville. Melbourne and Vancouver are in Trouville. Don't bother to go looking for what you can find on the spot. There are always on-the-spot places that are looking for movies; all you need is to see them.

You sometimes think that a given setting is going to help the movie. So you go looking for that setting and you never find it. You have to go scouting with nothing in mind, nothing. You have to let the exterior shots come to you. For example, I had no ideas about the image that should be under the hanged boy in Auschwitz. It was in going by the straight row of poplars in la Mauldre that I told myself: that's what it will be. Or else, it's the images seen without any film project in mind that come back to you. Like Le Poudreux, the port for African wood on the channel of the Seine and the run-down station in the old port of Honfleur.

A place where I've already done some shooting makes me want to return. I shoot in places where I've already made movies. The wide German skies in *Aurélia Steiner*, skies of fertile rains, they're the ones in *Le Camion* on writing and sleep—here they are fixed shots. Those fields were there, the difference was their color: they are black from the October ploughings in *Aurélia*, and covered again in *Le Camion* with that green January down. The difference was also in the light. Strong in *Aurélia*, milky in *Le Camion*. I dream about it, to shoot again in the places where I have made movies. In the Rothschild Palace and the park which is still inhabited by the beggar woman, the vice-consul's walks, crossing the deserted tennis courts. In my house. In the big empty lots in Auchan, the ones where the lady in *Le Camion* wanders, where she stops in the evening. For me these are the places that beget movies because movies have been made there. In Paris, too, I want to shoot on those great colonial avenues in *Les Mains négatives (Negative Hands)*, those Arab markets in Ménilmontant, that Mekong, to the east, in the vicinity of Bercy. The very image of Asia, I know where it is in Paris, before Renault, after the poplars on the Ile Saint-Germain, the piles of creeping vines, toward that jungle which borders Siam, before the lighthouse and the cemetery lantern.

THE YOUNG TIGHTROPE ARTIST FROM MONTREUIL IS THE RAGE OF PARIS. HE'S BEEN AT IT FOR TEN YEARS

(*France-Observateur*, the sixties)

—*Are you sometimes afraid?*

—I'm never afraid. My little niece, she's three, I sometimes take her with me on the wire; she's not afraid.

—*Does the net make a difference?*

—There are some departments where the net is required, others where it isn't allowed. For me, and for my father and mother, it makes no difference.

—*How high is the wire?*

—Twenty-five meters, the pole, forty meters. But with the pole I always work without a net. It's allowed. Like above rivers.

—*What were you doing before you came to Montreuil?*

—We weren't very far from Paris. We would hook the wire to a house and to a pylon on the other end. The wire was 390 meters long. I drove a motorcycle on it.

—*Without a net?*

—Yes. It was in a department that allowed it. I don't know anymore exactly where it was; there's a village called Sauvage. I'd go fishing, I like that.

—*What is the hardest thing you have done?*

—The day I crossed the Loire. It was very cold. We'd been waiting for three weeks. It was still just as cold so we had enough; I crossed. It was a long stretch, 500 meters. And the wire, in the middle, would jiggle at one meter's height, it's inevitable. I had to cross in wooden shoes. It was a bit difficult on the icy surface. But I did it.

—*Do you practice a lot?*

—Not in the summer. In the winter I practice every day, for three, four hours, with my father. You must never go for more than three days without practicing. I'm learning the double somersault on the wire; it's hard.

—*Is it the hardest?*

—No. The hardest is to walk on the wire on stilts. My father used to do it but he had an accident. But he'll teach me after the somersault.

—*Have you had time to go to school?*

—A priest, in Lyon, taught me to read, for three months. But I know how to speak French, English, and German.

—*Haven't you ever been afraid?*

—No, but at the top of the pole you have to be careful about the wind, it sways.

THE ANTELOPES

One day, on the Moroccan shores, a hundred and fifty years ago, thousands of antelopes together threw themselves into the sea. They drove each other on and they drowned. They came from all over Africa, from the forests, from the savannas, from the mountains; they gathered at the appointed place, on the appointed day, and they committed suicide. As they came from points that were at different distances from the gathering place, it was clear that they hadn't all set out the same day. They had to have started out at different times; for some the journey must have lasted several days, or several weeks; for others, months. The ones from Mozambique must have set out, let's say, in the last crescent moon of April, the ones from Guinea in full moon, in June. The visceral and sacred command that announced this day of reckoning was therefore very precise as to the day and the hour of their departure. Each one of them at the exact time, at the appointed hour, set out in the direction indicated, and this, apparently, according to a decision that must not have depended on any external signal but on the contrary, no mistake about it, on an individual desire. The decision here being obedience to the unknown of the law, but a decision as rash as choosing the savanna to act it out. Antelopes are not migratory; they are not a migrant species like storks, wild geese, or swallows. They were not at all accustomed to leaving their forest. They left it. It could be that for their species this perhaps involved a single command or various commands issued once every so many hundreds or even thousands of years in keeping with a rhythm unbeknownst to mankind. We don't know, of course. So they came out of the forest to take off in the direction of death. Not all the antelopes in Africa, only several thousand. Therefore, only certain ones set out, those appointed by the law. A nuance, but perhaps the most terrifying: only certain ones. This immutable logic of the species, this inscrutable pattern buried, submerged in the species, is as convincing as the grandiose, immeasurable ineptitude of life.

CHANGE

Books are selling well, relatively speaking, they sell more nowadays than tickets to movies. Publishing is picking up again. These days there is some recourse to reading, not, as some contend, to forget once more the notorious aggression of society of which cinema is an integral part, but simply to escape the worries you are thrown into by this worrisome combination: the aggression on one hand, as well as that shown by movies. On the other hand, people go much less to the movies these days. Before, we felt more or less obliged, we don't anymore. A lot of women. Young people too. A lot of film technicians. We go to see certain films, but not those that interest the critics. We are a handful and, for the most part, intellectuals, but it always starts like that, by a handful of intellectuals. Moreover, there are also those who are not buying, who are no longer watching, who no longer have, television.

CHANGE

It's going to last for a year and two months. We're going to see them every day. For four hundred days they will be imposed on us several hours a week. And we will pay the Dues. Our consolation is in knowing that millions of others are like us. We have in common an equivalent, identical animality; we are plunged into depression in the same way, and as far as we may be from one another, we find each other again, we live on the same earth, in the same country, with a different name: the new fraternity. One day, a man from Flanders and a man from Hungary discovered the most important change in the evolution of agriculture, the iron ploughshare. It was in the same era of human history.

JEAN PAULHAN,* READING MANUSCRIPTS
(1960, unpublished)

—Marguerite Duras. *Jean Paulhan, a great part of French literature has gone through your hands and still does, whether published or not. What do you learn from this experience?*

—*Jean Paulhan.* That literature, good or bad, is always useful; even when it is dreadful it shows growth in the author who creates it. I think that nothing should be completely discouraged in this regard.

It's in this sense that I had thought of publishing from time to time, obviously on bible paper, an anthology of all the manuscripts rejected during the year.

—*Isn't there such a thing as a completely dreadful, completely useless book?*

—I've never read one. Perhaps there are some, but I haven't read any. No, never. It seems to me that there is always something to get from a book.

—*Why do we write?*

* Author of books on psychology, philosophy, language, art, and poetry, Jean Paulhan was Director of the Nouvelle Revue Française from 1925 to 1940, and Co-Director, with M. Arland, from 1953 to 1968.

—I think that literature always teaches the one who is creating it to see himself and to see the world in a more precise or more complete way than he did up to then. It's very difficult to see the world and to see ourselves, and this for an extremely clear reason: when we look, we divert a part of our mind or our thought, so that what we then see is entirely false and conventional. Any kind of literature, even if it's very mediocre, very boring, is an effort to see the world as if we were not there. That is, after all, the goal of literature. That's what literature is after and what it attains, for everyone. But at any rate, for its author, even when it is mediocre or trivial, it has this result.

—*Does an author, even a completely solitary one, always have a reader: himself?*

—Always, and happily so. All literature brings us closer to the truth and brings its author closer to the truth, even if it seems hallucinatory because there is no completely hallucinatory literature. Or then, say that Lautréamont is the model of hallucinatory literature.

—*You are therefore using the word "literature" to refer to unpolished literature.*

—Yes. What is published assures—or we think that it will assure—a general growth for all readers, whereas unpublished literature, undoubtedly much more dreadful, only assures the growth of its author. But, after all, that's already a lot.

—*Is the fact that a book may only be "publishable" not the source of possible errors, as far as readers are concerned?*

—Yes. But the errors are very interesting. Often the reader, say the reader that I am, is amazed in reading a published book. He says to himself: "Why has the publisher published this?"

But that's what one says to oneself every day in seeing the books people are reading: "How the devil can this person read such a book?" It balances out. He's the one reading precisely the books that you don't want anything to do with. . . .

113

—If one were even more demanding, I think that instead of the two hundred novels that Gallimard publishes, out of the ten thousand manuscripts received, one ought to perhaps only publish barely fifty?

—Probably. But it should be pointed out that literary prizes have often been given to manuscripts rejected by all the publishers. When Bedel got the prix Goncourt for *Jérôme 60° latitude Nord* . . . I'm not sure anymore . . . that book had been rejected by all the publishers in Paris. It had gone back to Gaston Gallimard to whom Bedel had taken it, but quite as a last resort. And then, it got the prix Goncourt, which encouraged Gallimard, and, I think, all the publishers.

RAYMOND QUENEAU,[*] READING MANUSCRIPTS
(1960, unpublished)

—Marguerite Duras. *Raymond Queneau, how do you judge a manuscript to be good or bad?*

—*Raymond Queneau.* I don't think that you can judge the absolute quality of a manuscript. It is assessed from a particular point of view, the publisher's.

—Publishable or not?

—That's it. A question is then asked about the author: are we dealing with a writer, with a future writer, or else with someone who doesn't have a chance? We're not deciding so much whether

---

[*] Poet, novelist, author of *Zazie dans le metro* (1959), Queneau also served as Director of the Encyclopedia of the Pléiade for Gallimard.

a manuscript is good or bad, this is always very subjective. But we can see if the author of a manuscript belongs to the category of writers, of future writers, or else if he is simply an amateur. I think that one can rather quickly distinguish between the professional, the future professional, and the amateur.

When the professional submits a manuscript, he's not yet a professional writer, of course. But one feels, in reading it, that he is already conscious of what writing is, of what the craft and the work of the writer are, and that what he writes is destined to be published. Whereas the amateur—whose manuscript may be just as good or as bad—absolutely doesn't realize what literature and writing are; he is someone who thinks only of himself, who writes for his own pleasure, who writes to comfort himself. This is not far, if you will, from the diary of a girl who writes to relate her own feelings to herself. And from an author's first manuscript, one can guess if it's a hopeless matter of an amateur or else of someone who may become a writer, even if he must be a bad writer.

—*Could you say that an acrobat, a carpenter has anything in common with the good writer?*

—Yes. There are people who are carpenters or acrobats. They are perhaps bad acrobats or mediocre carpenters but they know their craft all the same. They aren't people who are Sunday painters, taking themselves for carpenters. The amateur writer is a dabbler, if you will.

A writer is someone who realizes that one doesn't write only to give pleasure to oneself, someone who is conscious of not being alone. The man, or the woman, who is truly concerned with writing knows he belongs to a community of other writers, that he has contemporaries who will judge him, who will criticize him, who will be writing in a parallel way. The amateur is unfortunately someone who stays in himself, who may write pleasant things, but who does not have the power necessary to communicate with others, with the public, even with a limited public. What has struck me most in the course of these years of reading manuscripts, is that one sees very quickly if an author, even totally unknown, already belongs, by vocation, in some way, to the guild of writers.

—*Is it rare?*

—Yes, very rare. Sometimes, this poses a problem. It happens that a manuscript is not good, although the author is clearly aware of what writing is. So, one hesitates to reject it.

—*That magic of publication, of the published work, can't anything take its place?*

—No, nothing. So, even if their manuscript isn't good, sometimes one hesitates to reject it. Often one may wonder if it wouldn't have been preferable to publish such a first manuscript, to turn it into a printed book, even not a very good one, even rather bad, because seeing the printed book, seeing one's writing in print, completely transforms the author. There is certainly a give and take between the printing, the first communication . . . with others, in short, a give and take with the readers.

—*On one hand it's a fascination, but also an objectification of the thing. Is it that a printed book can be seen better?*

—Yes. One says to oneself: "Here's an author . . . what he has written is not very good, but if he sees it in print, he will realize that it isn't good, he will feel the reactions of the public, of the readers, even if these readers are few, even if no one writes to him, even if he has no critics." The sole fact of knowing that there are, here and there, in the world, people who will read his book, will have an influence on him, will transform him, will help him to become aware of what writing is.

—*Can't a literary calling be belated? What do you think of the notary from the most secluded part of the Dordogne who, one fine morning, past fifty, starts to write a novel?*

—It happens, indeed. There are examples of writers who are late bloomers. But most often, it's a pathological sign. Almost always, a writer writes early, writes young.

—*At what age?*

—At seven. . . . Very young, in a word. . . . To my knowledge, most writers start writing when they are children. Almost all started at age seven, eight, ten.

—*When did* you *start to write?*

—I have no memory of not having written.

AURÉLIA AURÉLIA FOUR

Les Mains négatives and *Césarée* are rejected shots from *Le Navire Night (Night Ship)*. The statues of the [Place de la] Concorde and the Maillols were far too lavish for the kind of wasteland that *Le Navire Night* portrays. They were still too representational. Moreover, the shots from *Les Mains négatives*, from that dolly move that goes from the Bastille to the Champs-Elysées, were not good, for what technical reasons I don't know. The red lights are completely squashed, like blood stains, the picture is blurred. We did the shots over but I didn't use the new ones—except that stretch at the Magenta intersection, when you are in the cavernous, empty restaurants—I've kept almost all of the bungled shots.

We did the shooting in mid-August, Paris being relatively deserted for only one week a year. During the forty-five minutes of the dolly move between six-fifteen to a quarter to eight in the morning, aside from a prostitute on the boulevard Magenta, we met only some blacks, a few Portuguese maids near the Opera, the ones who clean the banks, some hoodlums too, and some homeless people. At that hour, Paris doesn't belong to us. And these people, the ones who clean the banks, the streets, the stores, completely disappear at eight o'clock; that's when we take possession of the place. Since Indochina, since my youth, I had never seen such an ethnic population gathered in a single spot. For sex, those are the ones you go to. There are old people too, a bum at the place de l'Opera. Puerto Ricans, mulattoes, before you get to the place du Palais-Royal. After that, there's nothing else, just garbage cans and cars.

I spent a month and a half on the text of *Aurélia Steiner Vancouver*—thirteen typed pages. I worked in Trouville. I'm best off there for writing. We did the shooting in four days. We had very little film stock, 72 minutes of film. One reel wasn't used. This left 68 minutes for shooting. The movie is exactly 50 minutes long. There are 18 minutes of rejected shots.

We shot *Aurélia Melbourne* against the light. The faces are erased, you see only their outline, the camera swallows them, the river takes them. I think that at one particular moment Aurélia is on a bridge. To the left of the picture, there is a silhouette of a girl with long blond hair. The face is blotted out like the others. She has a very lovely shape, tall, thin. No feature, but an Alice-in-Wonderland smile. This smile is all you see of the face. Yes, I think it's her too, Aurélia, she will never know it. She is there or somewhere else. She is broken into bits, scattered throughout the film. And fully there at the same time. She is still on the rue des Rosiers, first there, then somewhere else at the same time, always there, then, later, always some-where else, here as well as elsewhere, in all Jews: she is the first generation, like the last. She is writing. It's already almost forty years ago. She could not have been writing in '45. To do it, time has to pass over the horror. She is the leprous cat too, Aurélia

Steiner is. That Jew, that Jewish cat. Moreover, in those days, you would cross a Jewish continent. During that journey on the river in the north, Aurélia is calling her lover who has disappeared in the charnel houses, the wars, the crematories, the equatorial lands of hunger. We are exactly in the center of an unknown city where the river cuts through. The river would drain off all the Jewish dead and carry them away. They would be talking about Aurélia everywhere. You would hear her name whispered under the bridges, she would be in everyone's memory those days. Yes, the river would carry them away in the funeral bark toward the singular end of the river, to be diluted in the sea, throughout the universe. She is calling for help, Aurélia Steiner is, appealing to love while remembering. Calling from everywhere, remembering from everywhere. She is in Melbourne, Paris, Vancouver. From wherever there are dispersed Jews, refugees, she remembers. She can be only in places of this kind, where nothing happens except memory. Nothing happens in Melbourne, in Vancouver. And they are remote places. Far from Europe. I see them as survival places. They're white, white pages. Nothing happens there. The boredom of existing must be immeasurable. Recourse to other places, to other times must be constant. There are also Jews in Argentina. But they've been there for centuries. In Spain as well. There are no more Jews in Poland, there are no more in Germany. Within a certain time, there will be no more in Russia.

What does Jewishness represent in the non-Jew's private self-questioning? As opposed to what is this extreme recourse unlike anything else? What does it answer? What does it confirm?

It's something that is profoundly related to writing. The words that Aurélia Steiner utters at the end: "I am writing." Her cry isn't "I am calling" but "I am writing."

This has to do with God. Writing has to do with God.

Eighteen-year-old Aurélia Steiner, forgotten by God, sets herself up as equal to God face to face with herself.

Goldman was killed at the time I finished the first *Aurélia Melbourne*. I remember his saying, in an interview in *Le Monde*: "Our only homeland is writing, is the word." And I've been confirmed in what I see: this homeland without land, without a nation, is the most solid in the world, the most indestructible. Maybe the persecution of the Jews also comes from here: their land couldn't be taken away, they didn't have any, so for want of material to go after, they themselves got killed.

Take the name Steiner, since you have talked about Stretter; there is something that rhymes, also with Lol V. Stein.

Yes. Anne-Marie Stretter. The initials, almost the same ones.

Lol V. Stein, Jewess.

Yes, Jewess, I think. I think I don't ask myself the question in the book. The vice-consul, too, was Jewish. The vice-consul I knew, Jewish. He lived in Neuilly. He was vice-consul in Bombay. I remember, during the Vietnam War, they had discovered in the virgin forest, in Cambodia perhaps, I don't know anymore, a very old tomb that must have dated from the time of the conquest—the name was worn away, all you could read were the words, "Vice-consul of France."

Aurélia Steiner, how did she get to this point?

It's like the crime of writing; once you've done it you don't remember. Criminals say: 'I don't know what happened to me." I have a very slim point of departure. In my calendar—I've already mentioned it—a few words on how the sea looked one particular morning in July 1979.

Water plays a very important role in the four films.

You can't avoid preconceived ideas. I told Pierre Lhomme that the Seine in itself made no sense, that it was its banks that had to be filmed. That's how we lost a whole day of shooting. We threw away a day on point of view shots. The pictures took in too much of the banks. There was a little bit of Seine and a lot of banks. Whereas what was needed, what we'd decided on, was the fullness of the Seine, in its mass, in all its volume. And then, at random, there went by what went by, what came up got into the film: palaces, the Eiffel Tower, the Louvre, Notre-Dame, pleasure boats, guitars, shouts, trails along the banks, the evening, the lights. The focal point of the water, that was the focal point of the film. The convergence of these two points was the film. The banks, that was an entirely different film, a film about a river and not about death. I must say that Pierre Lhomme's work is not only very beautiful but of profound intelligence.

Michel Cournot saw in the film that water conveys eternity better than stone. Here, the water is completely walled in as it goes through the city. Its boundary, its bed are a construction; it is only after the river has gone beyond the city that it spreads out and rediscovers the fields, the woods.

STEINER

The first generation—the grandparents—were gassed at Auschwitz. They were Aurélia Steiner's grandparents. When that generation was exterminated they already had children. From the beginning of the war and even in the years preceding it, many of those children were sent away and entrusted to relatives who lived far from Europe, the aunts and the uncles of Aurélia Steiner's parents. The last Aurélia was therefore born abroad, in Melbourne and in Vancouver. I don't think she ever went back to Europe. Aurélia Steiner, like all the Jews of Israel or of Europe, through her parents and her grandparents, is therefore a survivor of the camps, an oversight, an accident in the generalization of death. It must also be said that fifty or so Jewish children were born and grew up in Auschwitz, hidden under the partitions. Some of them were found, those who survived were sent to a psychiatric hospital in England. None of them was familiar with the use of the first person singular. They would say *"wir,"* "we." Aurélia Steiner did not invent the birth of the child in Auschwitz.

There is a relationship among your films in general by a certain proximity to water, to the sea, to a city cut through by a body of water or in contact with water. Anne-Marie Stretter is from Venice, she goes to Calcutta, it's in the sea that she drowns. Inversely, Aurélia is very far away, she is defined by a tragic immobility, an exile.

She is in the concentration camps, that is where Aurélia Steiner lives. The German concentration camps, Auschwitz, Birkenau, were continental locations, stifling, very cold in winter, scorching in summer, very deep into the interior of Europe, very far from the sea. It's there that she goes to write her story, that is, the story of the Jews of all time.

ÉDOUARD BOUBAT

If eyes could see what Boubat's photography sees, could they bear it? I'm thinking of certain photographs of children. Of children who suddenly discover they are being photographed and are divided between the fear, the wonder, the initial amazement of "why us and not others?," "us rather than something else?" I'm thinking too about certain landscapes of foreign lands, of harvests, photos of girls dressed for first communion, and about a host of moments whose meaning is impossible to put into words, to put into a title—moments snatched from the passage of days so like other days, as well as from the passage of lifetimes—thinking about moments full of light, about the flash of an inexplicable happiness, impossible to name, as fleeting as the wind—about mysterious movements in certain places, at certain hours, in deserted landscapes or at the edge of twilights of love's paralyzing breath. Boubat's photography—in particular his photos of women—always acts in a range that goes beyond what it represents. While it bears witness to the most irreplaceable quality in the identity of a face, by the same token it bears witness to the fragility of this identity and its mortal nature. To what is not replaceable and which nevertheless is lost in a universal morphology. When Édouard Boubat captures the inevitable uniqueness of a face, it would seem that it is always at the very moment when it is least expected, the moment when the face loses its identity to blend into what exists at the same time, near or far from it, somewhere else, or next door, or lost, or dead. Édouard Boubat told me one day that photography had a mystery of its own. He said, too, that there was in photography a truth that bore no resemblance to anything else, not to cinema, not to writing, nor painting. But that all this was for others to discover, not photographers. What I think is revealed here is that all photography is in one way or another your own. That there is no photography that does not bear witness to what is in you.

THE IDEA OF GOD

To the extent that cinema exists only relatively to other things, science, oil, money, you can talk about it indefinitely without getting anywhere at all in other domains. You can be very well acquainted with the cinema, its history, its sequences, without getting anywhere else at all, just staying with it. With very rare exceptions like Ordet, *for example, which reaches through a film one of the extremes of faith, which through a film shows the overpowering, unapproachable force of the idea of God.*

WONDERFUL MISERY

Would you accept a sort of concert where people would come together just to hear your voice? What fascinated me is what you were saying one day about the performance of James where the stage would extend to the back of the theater.

Yes, I remember, you would hear the actors speaking well before seeing them, they would come closer to us little by little. Are you thinking of the voice and a bare screen?

No, no screen at all. It's funny, at the Action-République I had the impression that people were going to a reading.

It's hard to answer that. When I speak I'm not facing you, I am with the text, alone with it.

One has the impression that what interests you in cinema is how words come to you — the process.

I slow down the reading a lot. In *Aurélia Steiner Vancouver*, it was supposed to last an hour to account for the forty days it took to write it.

You once said that to write was a "wonderful misery." I wonder if what you hate in Communism is that they will never admit that writing can be solitary and on the other hand, a joy.

I don't hate them. I look forward to their death. It's true, their domain is in fact a domain where writing doesn't occur, doesn't have a place. It's known that people paint, people write in the hiding places of big Russian cities, like criminals. Among the militants I've known, I've rarely encountered readers of books, I've only encountered readers of required readings, nobody else. In the Stalinist parties, what would be one's point of departure for reading, for writing? — yes, insubordination, true. Since that — the point of departure for those who used to write in bourgeois societies — has been poisoned, destroyed, one cannot, so they think, begin all over again without being an offender, an anti-revolutionary. To write, that was like reading, being suspect of betraying the people, tantamount to taking out of their hands a part of man's freedom. It was a theoretical crime. They considered writers and readers the way men previously had viewed witches, hundreds of years ago. The writer, in their eyes, was a feminine being prone to ambiguity, to a profound duality capable of undermining the purity of the general rule, the official rule of mental health. Ambiguity, duality, the most suspect words of all, they don't hear them, don't understand them. The rule was and still is literalness.

The most amazing of all these amazing things is still that this has never changed, that it never changes, never in any way,

never. This is perhaps the greatest disaster. Hearing Ellenstein talk about his membership in the Communist Party is like having a terrifying, pitiful dream of history repeating itself. Similarly, between the articles in *Pravda* nowadays and the tenor of a Section Committee newspaper twenty years ago, there isn't a shade of anything new unless it's the vocabulary, the syntax. For fifty years they've been going around in circles in the Soviet cellar, a place with no air, no openings. Yes, today they would still be indignant to see Riva making love with a German in *Hiroshima mon amour.*

Would the wonderful misery you were talking about perhaps be that of communication?

No. To write is not to be able to avoid doing it, not to be able to escape it. It concerns the individual alone. As for the rest,

whether the book communicates something makes no difference. I don't see the writer writing to try to establish this communication with other people through the book. I see him as
prey to himself, in those shifting grounds bordering upon those
of passion, impossible to pin down, to see, and from which
nothing can free him. You are there at the end of the world, at
the limits of yourself, incessantly feeling yourself on strange
ground, constantly approaching something without getting there.
For you don't get there just as in the unbearable aspects of desire
and passion. Writings that seem the most polished are but very
distant faces of what has been glimpsed, that inaccessible totality
which escapes all understanding, which yields to nothing but
madness, to what destroys it. But to give, give *yourself*—it's
probably that too—this effort worked out in a dark room you do
not enter but whose existence you have sensed, if only once,
through the transports and ebbing of desire. The wonderful
misery is perhaps that torture, that entreaty which allows no
respite, that uprooting of self which leaves you forsaken and lost
when it ends with the book. You know too. To be the object of
one's own madness and not go mad, that could be it, the wonderful misery. All the rest is beside the point.

THERE ARE NO COMMUNIST WRITERS

Did your belonging to the P.C.F. ever change what you wrote?
It's one of the things that makes me believe I'm a writer.
Does that mean you've never been a Communist writer?
No, it means that I have been a writer. There are no Communist writers. Someone said: experience shows that the fact of being a Communist seems to have killed the fact of being a writer.
Aragon . . .
No. It's not in the context of his belonging to the party that he was a writer, he was a writer before then, well before. He's a man who writes remarkably well but that's all. He's no longer topical. He's been retired into the historical novel. He bears a certain resemblance to the narrators of official events in Soviet history who have kept to the style of the exhaustive account, just like the Soviet cinema. He no longer changes anything. He no longer sparks the writing of others.

I saw three of his interviews on television, I had a great deal of contempt for him, the man, but I had never seen him. On his face he wore the sort of lie of which I suspected him, a talent for pretending to be in good faith, to be almost naive, in order to make you swallow his lies, and now these things can be seen, they are seen better than before, with our getting to know the human face on television. And with Aragon, everyone saw it, everyone saw the lie; it made you very uncomfortable. I remember having lowered my eyes in shame when he spoke of the human lives he had saved.
Was it a mask?
No, not a mask. Worse than a mask. His face had become a mask, but a living one. A horrible one. He was lying all the time and all over the place. Not only in the account of his merits but in his very language. The words didn't ring true, they didn't

shine, as if abashed. It reached the point of being disgusting for those who are used to this. His eyes, like Marchais, were unseeing. He went on talking without anyone stopping him. I was hoping someone would say: you're lying, a technician, for instance, one of the viewers there during the shooting. No. No. They heard out this slimy hero to the end. But many, many people finally understood that night what Aragon was.

NAUSEA

I see that power of whatever kind, the power of the people or of a faction, is always a nauseating episode in the history of man and of the world. In every case the taking of power is usurpation of the power that preceded it. The word for legality applied to incumbent power ought to evoke comedy. I think that the power of poverty is as insane as that of money, as that of faith. That the young hired killers of Pierre Goldman are as sickening as the ones who pay them. I believe that poverty which claims the right to judge and to punish, to kill, whether in the name of justice, of faith, or of force, becomes strictly like the power of money that it has just overthrown. That it readjusts to it, *replaces* it. That the execution of the Afghan thieves in Teheran in December 1979 carries on the executions ordered by the Shah, the ones ordered by Hitler, Stalin, Pinochet. That in every one of us, that in every nation, at every moment, we have what it takes to make a Hitler, a Stalin, a Shah, a Pinochet. In a hundred years we have been for several weeks without any power in France, a few months in 1870, a couple of weeks in 1968. As if the history of France had all of a sudden surrendered to nonsense. Then all of a sudden, men got scared of this undefined state.

CINEMA, NO

Many people will think that I'm "off track" in talking about cinema. That I don't have a good grasp of what I'm talking about when I talk about cinema. I say that everyone can talk cinema. Films are there and they're being made. Nothing pre-exists films. Most of the time people want to make them because the practice of filmmaking doesn't require any special gift, it's a bit like handling an automobile. The majority of books are done that way. But they aren't confused with other books, the ones that are done in ignorance of the laws of the genre. But for cinema, one sometimes errs, by mistaking *Cahiers du Cinéma* for *Tel Quel*, like taking *Cries and Whispers* for a porno film.

One thinks up writing on one's own. Everywhere. In no matter what case. Cinema, no. Films do not call. They do not await like the written work, that great rush into the book. When no one makes films, films do not exist, have never existed. When no one writes, the written work still exists, it has always existed. When everything is over, on the dying world, the gray planet, it will still exist everywhere, in the air of time, on the sea.

WHY MY FILMS?

When I go to the movies, I lose sight of myself once more, I don't exist anymore, maybe this is why people don't want to go anymore. In the space of your films I am always there.

The problem is to know why, why my films. All the reasons I've been giving for years are vague, I don't manage to see it

132

clearly. It must concern my own life. When I have talked about it, it was often to say that it was difficult for me to grasp. Maybe it's the longing to "paste written texts" on pictures. Or else, quite simply, it's that space of the cinema that attracts me, the space of the movie house, that point of convergence.

I would make a distinction between a public reading of your texts and a projection of a dark film in a darkened theater accompanied by your texts.

Yes, the arrangement of the seats makes it different. They are all turned toward the same space, the picture's space. And in a theater, the voice is all around you, the film projects it all around. If someone gives a reading in a house, we are around him. In a darkened theater with a dark screen, people would still look at the screen; they would know where their eyes should go, where to direct their look. In a living room with people, they wouldn't know where to look, what they should focus on.

There's also this, something subversive about the cinema you do because it doesn't resemble any other cinema, and I had the impression at the Action-République that the people who were there were of kindred spirit, whom you were bringing together for this kind of cinema. That there was something in the air coming from a new public that would enjoy a like community of mind and interests. I was amazed at not knowing the viewers who were there with me.

I've already had this feeling in certain movie houses, for example in Digne which for me is one of the meccas of cinema. And I was told that in Paris, after the last showing of *Le Camion*, the audience didn't leave right away; they stayed together and talked among themselves.

What you're saying is good, very good. The fact that people put classified ads in *Libération* saying they have mini-cassette tapes of my texts available, the way they sell porno films, this would go in the direction you're suggesting, of subversion.

Provocation also interests you.

Yes. To know how far I'm going to be able to go. Also to put to the test this rotten thing we call cinema.

Every word you write is a challenge. The same for the movies you make.

Even so, there's a curious thing. Talkies appeared around 1930. What is the first movie whose lines people repeat? It is Hiroshima mon amour. People weren't very interested in the sound in movies. From what other movies were sentences, dialogues quoted?

There was Prévert.

. . . .

Yes, but there it was words more than sentences. Now it is developed in all your films.

. . . .

Boulez was saying the other day: "In films, the music annoys me because it is never thought out in relation to the film. If you have to choose, I prefer Vivaldi to Tiomkin because during that time, I'm listening to Vivaldi. If I were making a film, I would try to completely conceive the music with the one who is making the film. That has only been done once, when Prokofiev and Eisenstein made Ivan the Terrible, and still, the result isn't brilliant.

. . . .

We have the impression that silent movies are self-evident, that your cinema is self-evident, then that between the two, it's no longer so self-evident. . . .

In commercial cinema, speech takes the picture forward; it often economizes the sequence of pictures. If someone says: I'm going to see my fiancée, this makes the sequence more economical.

. . . .

Speech is something else entirely in your films.

. . . .

That's why you could make India Song and Son nom de

Venise dans Calcutta desert (Her Name of Venice in Calcutta Desert), *with the same sound tape. Why, but why, didn't anyone dare to do it before, it's so obvious.*

. . . .

Something general is that one constantly wants to quote you, including the intonations of your voice.

When I speak I have the same voice as in films. I've been told this.

There's an intonation to your voice and inflections that are recognizable and that correspond to the way you accentuate the text, to the syntax, and to invocatory patterns. That is, you often soliloquize dialogues: "She says this."

. . . .

And it's important on the level of what is happening between the characters; on the level of what Aurélia Steiner has the sailor do, there's always something like a challenge.

When I speak, I have a negative concern, I'm taking care not to move away from the neutral ground where all words are equal. They come and I'm obliged to take them and make them public. I make them go from one place to another, I take them from sleep, I put them in the daylight, without making a fuss.

When you say: "You see," to whom are you speaking?

I'm saying this to someone. Those texts, I began by telling to someone.

One could make a film like that which would be the projection of a manuscript.

No. A manuscript isn't neutral. It's what cannot be seen.

THE WRITTEN IMAGE

When I see a written text in Aurélia Steiner, *I want to see the original text. More than the image.*

The written image. "I can do nothing about the eternity that I bring to the place you last looked upon—the white rectangle in the courtyard where the prisoners of the camp are assembled." Already in *Night*, sentences were first spoken and then seen in writing.

In the book Aurélia Steiner, *one sees the progression of each text leading to the other. The cry in the night in* Le Navire Night. *Afterwards, the cry cutting across geography. Then in the caves and then in time.*

I don't see anything equivalent to the space of the white rectangle of death. It's a space to be filled, to refill, and it's the place where Aurélia Steiner was born.

This place is in every life and that is why this white rectangle has a universal value.

No. No, the Jewish place, I can't manage to resolve it, to connect it, even very distantly to a basic element in our life. The mystery remaining for me is only this: that there are people who do not see it the way I see it. At a certain moment, I say: "The public square is empty except for your body." I hear: "History is empty except for your death." The death of a Jew in Auschwitz, as far as I'm concerned, fills the entire history of our times, the whole war.

You see the white rectangle as having specific reference to the history of the Jews?

Yes, no extermination has been on the order of that of the Jews, none, in the history of the world. It isn't a genocide. It isn't a punitive crusade, an outburst of violence. It's a decree, a deliberate decision, a logical organization, a meticulous, fanatical prediction of the removal of a race of men. I recall for the nth time the existence of those female stranglers, of those Women's Corps, of the Agents for the Strangling of Jewish Children. In the same way there was the Teaching or Medical Corps.

What's mysterious is that image of the white rectangle. That hole.

It's a page too, a scene. Originally it was my personal translation of Elie Wiesel's book, *Night*. He tells about the death of a little thirteen-year-old Jew who was so thin, so weightless, that he couldn't manage to hang himself and was kicking for three days at the end of his rope in the courtyard of the camp. This intolerable image of all time I see this way: under the body of the child, I see a white rectangle. It is paved, perfect, bare, no one goes near the child during his death agony. The Swiss border routes are also, for me, white rectangles. The Jewish parents would take their children—in the night—on those routes; they would make them cross over to the Swiss soldiers and would run away.

I believe that the Jews, this turmoil for me so powerful, and which I see in an absolute light, which I face in a killing clearsightedness—this meets what I write. To write is to go

looking outside of oneself for what is already inside oneself. One function of this turmoil is to put together in a new way the latent horror spread out over the world, which I recognize. It makes one see the principle of the horror. The word Jew, at the same time, speaks of the power of death that man may grant himself and its recognition by us. It's because the Nazis did not *recognize* this horror in them that they committed it. The Jews, this turmoil, this déjà vu, must certainly have begun—for me— with my childhood in Asia, with the lazarettos outside the villages, the endemic diseases of plague, cholera, poverty; the condemned streets of those stricken with the plague are the first concentration camps I saw. Then, I blamed God.

You described yourself with your brother as "thin and yellow" children, and racially different from your mother.

Yes, we didn't have her skin color, we weren't afraid of either heat or sun, we would run away all the time to join the children of the forest villages.

BEACHES

The other day, I said to you: how you must have suffered to write what you write. And you said: yes, I had to suffer.

But I think it's like this, that unhappiness is recorded. I had to experience unhappiness as a natural state. All women must have suffered without knowing it. When they tell you: how happy I was in such and such a year, we went on vacation to Biarritz, the children were little, etc. It's not true. Not true. The man is the one who was dictating that fake happiness, who was saying: aren't things great today, my dear, the weather is beautiful. . . . The man was taking a rest from work. We didn't need that, not anything like it, but on the contrary to leave, to explode that fakery. Compelled to, we would relax. The beaches would drive us crazy with boredom.

Is this awareness in happiness something that women possess and men do not?

No. They had and still have every opportunity to transgress it, by leaving. A new mistress, a new love, is going a lot farther than a trip around the world. We, for the most part, would stay home. I have the impression of having written in my kitchen, while cooking. But I am also capable of writing instead of keeping myself alive, forgetting to eat. That happened while I was doing *Aurélia Steiner*.

WE WOMEN ARE ALL ACQUAINTED
WITH SORROW

The other day, you said: "We women are all Aurélia Steiner, we are all fierce, we are all of us acquainted with sorrow." Those words touched me deeply and then I wondered why you said "we women" and not just "all of us."

Because I think that we women are all [affected], and not all men. Sorrow, for men, up to now, throughout time, throughout history, has always found its outlet, its solution. It was transformed into anger, into external events, like war, crimes, turning women out, in Moslem countries, in China, burying adulterous women with their lovers, both alive, or disfiguring them. When I was five years old, in Yunnan they were still burying lovers alive, face to face in the casket. The deceived husband was the sole judge of the punishment. We have never had any other recourse but muteness. Even so-called liberated women, by their own declaration. One cannot compare woman's experience of sorrow with man's. Man cannot bear sorrow, he palms it off, he has to get away from it, he projects it outside of himself in hallowed, ancestral demonstrations which are his recognized transfers—battle, outcries, the show of discourse, cruelty.

WOMEN AND HOMOSEXUALITY

I see a relation between homosexuality and women's movements. They are, similarly, first and foremost preoccupied with themselves. Even pointless remarks made against homosexuality have the effect of strengthening their position in this minority separatism, paradoxically painful and desired. Today, one could say that women are intent upon still keeping intact and whole their difference with men. In the same way that homosexuals want to stick to the old tyranny, to keep the whole distance between them and society. To dare to suggest that things are improving for them is to offend them greatly. Like women, homosexuals want to keep open the legal actions brought against man, against society. They institute these actions, they make them the context for belonging, the chosen context of their martyrdom. I think that in avoiding militancy, women would have evolved in the same way. One sees these things from one's own perspective. I have not been an activist in any women's movement—the idea still makes me run—and I have changed just like them, perhaps more, forever. I could say: in my past. I see my life now. I didn't used to see it. I see it with great amazement, increasing amazement.

I WONDER HOW

I wonder how I endured so much kindness, so much concern, so much profound affection, protection, so much pity, so much putting me to sleep, so very much advice, how I stayed there, with them, without ever running away. How I am not dead. All the vacations with them, the same man, the same men, every summer, the summer evenings, with them, the same one, the same ones, love, travels, sleep, music, for years and years closeted with the same one, the same ones. The pain, the agonizing betrayals, with no tomorrow, the watchfulness, pain enough to make you yell, keeping your silence, and why? Taken to Venice, taken care of, much admired, so that I forget the separation, taken away half-dead by force, worshipped, were I a thousand years old I could not bear separation, they all make it a point to tell me that it must be. Why? A wasted, aborted life. This straight line in the life of all women, this silence about the story of women. This failure which would make one believe in a happy ending. This happy ending which does not exist, which is a desert.

THE ILLNESS OF INTELLIGENCE

Couldn't you also say of Aurélia Steiner as of the vice-consul that her illness is intelligence?
Yes, I could. Couldn't you?
Yes.
But an intelligence without a cure.
Literally, an insane intelligence.
Out of control.
She is insane, too, Aurélia Steiner is, in a certain way.
Yes, she set off in madness. Like Abraham. She is someone who has gone off. She will not stop, Aurélia Steiner.
Is she the same one in Paris, Melbourne, and Vancouver?
Yes, she's the same one. At the same time. At every age. I can show you her photograph, as a child. I found her, Aurélia, at Neauphle. She was seven. She is not in the film but even so she was filmed. We didn't know how to film her with Pierre Lhomme, we didn't know how to capture her wildness. There is no difference between Aurélia's eyes and the sea, between her penetrating look and the depth of time.

AT THE MOVIES

At the movies, people are won over, captured. You can always say that they are predisposed, that you start with a ready-made public.

Even with that, you would hear sounds of fidgeting. Don't we hear people fidgeting?

No, there's a captive effect. I think that your voice, the way your voice resonates over the images, is of major importance in this process. We are captured by a voice. You were saying that Aurélia Steiner is calling. That appeal is spelled out this way: "I am writing." There's no difference to be made. This text is a voice *and this voice is a text. Then, one of two things: either this stream of words breaks off and the machine is jammed, or it doesn't break off and we are carried to the end. In this case, it doesn't break off. The text runs on.*

I think there is no hiatus, no blank space between the voice and what it is saying. When I am speaking, I am Aurélia Steiner, if you will. What I'm careful about is less, not more. It is not to convey the text but to be careful not to get away from her, Aurélia, who is speaking. It takes extreme care, every second, not to lose Aurélia, to stay with her, not to speak in my name. To respect Aurélia even if she comes from me.

Since this question of the face has been raised, I think that Aurélia Steiner's mobile face takes shape gradually. At the same time that we are taking in the story, the text your voice.

The most fitting term would perhaps be coalescence, osmosis. It's hard to imagine that someone else could recite this text. You were Aurélia Steiner at the same time you were writing it and reading it. You are Aurélia Steiner. We don't think: this is Marguerite Duras. I don't see someone other than you being able to utter this text. Perhaps it's a delusion.

Actually, what we can say is that your cinema apparently, absolutely transgresses all conventional ideas about cinema. That, for example, everything should appear to happen through the movements of the image, through the intervention of the image. You do the opposite, or in any case, there are, it seems, two parallel streams, necessary and unpredictable at the same time, constantly accidental: the stream of words and the stream of images. I'm thinking rather of Césarée, *or of* Les Mains néga-tives, *equally of* Aurélia Steiner Vancouver *where the image, in a certain way, is much more planned.*

There was all the same a margin between the texts in *Césarée*, in *Les Mains négatives*, and my emotion, my movement. There is no more margin in my passion for Aurélia and the text. At the end, in Vancouver, I am Aurélia. In the Paris text, when Aurélia is seven, with bombs falling overhead, in that black tower, in the middle of the forest, I am Aurélia too. The leprous cat in the dark cave, the Jewish cat who rejoins the beggar woman of Calcutta, the cat under the bridges dying of hunger that she lets die. I come together with it too, as does Aurélia.

MAKING AND GOING TO MOVIES

*Something is happening nowadays which is quite noticeable:
it's very rare that movies are exciting. In your movies there is an
excitement. I don't know if the term is quite right. It's something
I've also felt, in a general way, in seeing* Aurélia Steiner, *it's that
it makes movies exciting, as it were. You can also say that there's
a cruelty which comes through. On a multiple level.*

Love.

They are always cruel loves.

They weren't of my choosing.

THE OTHER CINEMA

Isn't what you do another kind of cinema?

Yes, I think so. I also know it by myself. When I don't
succeed in resolving my films in the traps of cinema, when they
remain open-ended like constant questions, when I cannot free
myself from their thought, it's because I have made films. This
is where I've been since I did the *Aurélia Steiner* films.

148

149

THE TREMULOUS MAN
(Conversation with Elia Kazan
Hotel de Crillon, December 1980*)

Marguerite Duras. *I want to distribute* Wanda, *your wife, Barbara Loden's film. I am not a distributor. I mean something else by this word, I mean to use all my energy to make certain that this movie reaches the French public. I believe I can. I think that there is a miracle in* Wanda. *Usually there is a distance between the visual representation and the text, as well as the subject and the action. Here this distance is completely nullified; there is an instant and permanent continuity between Barbara Loden and* Wanda.

Elia Kazan. Her acting career showed her that no script was permanent. For her, there was always an element of improvisation. (I am speaking English in order to be more precise.) There was always an element of improvisation, a surprise, in what she was doing. The only one, as far as I know, who was like that is Brando when he was young. He never knew exactly what he was going to say, therefore everything would come out of his mouth very alive.

—*The miracle for me isn't in the acting. It's that she seems even more herself in the movie, so it seems to me—I didn't know her—than she must have been in life. She's even more real in the movie than in life; it's completely miraculous.*

—It's true. She had great difficulty in communicating, except in moments of strong feeling, passion or rage, sexual passion, anger, etc., when the controls would snap. In some way there was an invisible wall between her and the world, but her work

*The meeting between Duras and Kazan was arranged for *Cahiers du Cinéma* by Serge Daney and Jean Narboni, who were present, as well as Dominique Villain and Michael Wilson, who translated.

permitted her to make some openings in this wall. She would do this every time. She played with me in the theater in a play by Arthur Miller; I don't like the play but there was one good thing in this play: what Barbara did.

—*What play?*

—*After the Fall.*

—*I haven't seen it. I'm insisting because I was very moved by her being herself in her movie. It's as if she had found a way in the movie to make sacred what she wants to portray as a demoralization, which I find to be an achievement, a very, very powerful achievement, very violent and profound. That's the way I see it.*

—In this movie she plays a character we have in America, and who I suppose exists in France and everywhere, that we call *floating,* a wanderer. A woman who floats on the surface of society, drifting here or there, with the currents. But in the story of this movie, for a few days the man she meets needs her; during these few days she has a direction and at the end of the movie, when he dies, she goes back to her wandering. Barbara Loden understood this character very, very well because when she was young she was a bit like that, she would go here and there. She once told me a very sad thing; she told me: "I have always needed a man to protect me." I will say that most women in our society are familiar with this, understand this, need this, but are not honest enough to say it. And she was saying it sadly.

—*Personally—this is getting a little beyond the subject—I feel very close to her. Like her I'm acquainted with the cafes, the last ones open, where you linger without any other reason but to while away the time, and I'm very well acquainted with alcohol, very intensely, the way I'd be acquainted with someone.*

—You know, *Wanda* is a movie that was made with no money. With $160,000, which doesn't pay the salaries of a big crew for a week. I was there all the time during the shooting; I

took care of the children, I played nursemaid. The crew con-
sisted of a cameraman, a sound engineer, a technician, an
assistant, and, on occasion, me.

—(Laughter.) *I'm familiar with this kind of production.*

—It's what I love, shooting with friends. Some time ago I
made a movie like that, *The Visitors*, with no money. But no
one came to see it; very few people in America, except in
colleges.

—*There is a public for* Wanda. *Perhaps America is uncivilized
in a way that I'm not very familiar with, that I haven't explored.
But what I do know is that there is a public for this movie. It's
simply a matter of finding it, of letting it know that this film
exists. If I let them know, since the cinema I do is on that track,
in that same off-beat split, they will come the way they come to*

see my movies. I want to make it clear that my doing this has nothing to do with her being a woman and my being a woman. If a man had made this movie, I would stand up for him in the same way.

—I understand. You are a sensitive person, you respond to Barbara, to Barbara's honesty. I'm delighted. I'm going to call Diamantis who has the movie in France; don't worry, it will work. This is so important for me. I'm trying to do something in America, too.

—*Why did I have this feeling that you I would never know?*

—But you have always known me!

—*I think of you as someone very far away. You live in a kind of America I don't see.*

—I live outside of New York, away from the society of movie-makers, authors, theater people. I have to say, too, that I spend half my time in the country, where I have a house.

—*You've never lived in Turkey?*

—Yes, as a child and I went back four or five times.

—*How old were you when you came to America?*

—Have you read the article I wrote on the Turkish prisons? I have it upstairs. I think it would interest you. I wrote that article in reaction to *Midnight Express*, which I found racist. I visited a friend in prison, a very good Turkish filmmaker, Guney, a very good friend of mine. My account of that visit was published in the *New York Times Magazine* and in *Positif* in French. I love Turkey, it's very wild, the interior is primitive.

—*But it's you who are the wild one. You are a savage.*

—Me? Yes. Turkish men are a little like the Japanese or the Mexicans. They have a side that says, "I love you, I adore you," and another side . . . "Grrrr . . ." that's very dangerous!

—*That's called versatility in French.*

—They aren't civilized.

—*I wanted to talk to you about* America, *which I saw again*

*because I knew I was going to meet you. Coming out of the movie
I was saying, "There are two great movies about exile"—I don't
mean emigration—"Chaplin's movie and* America, *Kazan's*
America.*"*

—They're the only ones? Why? It's the most important thing
about America.

—*Yes, but America is exile.*

—But why? Why aren't there other movies on immigration?
I don't understand. There's a Swedish movie by Jan Tröll but it's
too romantic a movie for me.

—*But I think that your movie is not a movie on immigration.
I think it covers a territory much more vast than that.*

—I was hoping that was the case.

—*Stavros, I think, stands for all of you. You're talking about
a much more fundamental, much more universal exile than an
exile motivated simply by conditions of poverty, the kind of exile
that goes from rags to riches, in other words, from central Europe,
from the Middle East to America. It goes much further than that.*

—I was hoping it would be universal. My idea was that, in
order to get to America, Stavros would have to give up a bit of
his honor, a bit of his belonging to the clan, and he never stops
saying one untrue thing. He says: "In America I will be white-
washed." And at a certain moment in the movie he says to the
girl, "Don't trust me, don't trust me." Because by then he knows
his weakness.

—*It's the moment you really get to Stavros in the movie. There
he is, as if stopped.*

—The best text in the movie is when he says, "Don't trust
me." He loves the girl, but he tells her, "Don't trust me."

—*It's sublime. But you know that Stavros is going to leave
America too. That he will never stop.*

—That's my next book. I'm in the process of writing it. He's
been living over there for nine years and at the end of the ninth

year, he has become a monster—because of the anger, the disappointment, the rejection, all those forces that are in America, which I felt when I was young. When I was young, I was becoming violent, violent. I was like an animal when I entered college, I didn't trust anyone. I'm in the process of writing this now.

—*If you will, the radical difference between you and the others who make movies in America, I'm not saying the Americans, I don't know what this means in cinema, I know that there's a place called Hollywood, a place called New York, but the difference between the others and you . . .*

—I'm not from Hollywood. . . .

—*. . . it's that fundamental wildness one recognizes in all your movies, which is like your signature.*

—Thank you. I still have it, I still feel it.

—*Which is like the name of your country.*

—(In French) I adore you . . . you really understand me! When someone understands me, suddenly my French comes back. . . . I'm not American, I'm not Turkish, I'm not Greek . . .

—*I'm in your situation. I was born in the Colonies. My birthplace is demolished. And if you will, that, that is always with me—the fact that one doesn't live where one was born.*

—To be denaturalized is to be castrated, to lose one's power. When you adapt to society, when you say, "I accept what they are," you have no more power left. Anger is often very important, it saves your life.

—*But you are never cut off from your childhood. It's not because you move around that you are cut off from your childhood.*

—More than roots, anger itself, the anger you feel when you are young.

—*Yes. The capacity for anger.*

—The response of anger to what is around you. This can be interpreted in a number of ways; it's the feeling of anger that is important. If not, you may die. I mean, men who become impotent, sexually impotent, sometimes they become this way because they no longer have any feelings in them. It's symbolic of another impotence.

—*But I consider us the lucky ones.*

—I think so, too.

—*To have been cut off from the mythology that is childhood, from one's native land.*

—I've noticed that among creative people, many have been moved early in their lives from one place to another, transplanted. So they had to adjust, to become acclimatized like a plant, like a tree and to become extremely strong. . . . France is an irresistibly bourgeois country: so much comfort, so much good food, so many cheeses, good wines, fruits, vegetables . . .

—*But America too . . .*

—Yes, America too. But all the same, France is so comfortable. America also means television, automobiles, cinema, etc.

—*Let's continue talking about childhood. We had two chances, poverty and the distance of the place where we lived later on. I consider these two chances. You were able to return to Turkey. For me, there was the war, I was married, I had a child. I never could and I never will return to my native land. I am completely separated from my childhood. And it is there, in all my books, in all my movies, childhood is there. I think that the people who are with us, these friends, who were all born in France, in accessible countries, cannot understand this situation, to be without a native land. I don't feel French. Are you American?*

—I don't feel Greek, I don't feel American. . . . Now I feel I come from everywhere, a citizen of the world. I'm romantic in my connection to poor people, to the working class, to bohemians. They are everywhere in the world and I feel close to them. I have a snobbish attitude with regard to the rich and those who are lucky.

—*What I wanted to add earlier on when I was talking about*

the territory of your movies, about the territory that you approach and in which you work, it's that you are perhaps the only international American filmmaker. The territory in which you work is international in nature.

—I think that's true, I hope it's true. It's the way I feel. I feel as much at home here as in America, in Greece, or in Turkey. I am also the only Greek who loves Turkey. I have a very good Greek friend who hated me because of the article I was telling you about, because I showed the Turks as human beings. He's one of my best friends and he got angry with me. He came to my office; he told me, "I hated that article," he left and I didn't see him again for a year. And that article was only treating the Turks as humans.

—*So, you do have relations with Turkey on a regular basis?*

—I went back there in 1956 for *America*. If I had a whole evening, I could tell you loads of stories about Turkey, about that trip, about everything.

—*Which one of your movies is your favorite?*

—My favorite movie is *America, America*.

—*I am crazy about one part, I'm not saying the whole movie, of* Wild River. *I think that the love story between Lee Remick and Montgomery Clift must be among the greatest ever filmed. Perhaps the greatest, it could be the most beautiful. I may be going to shock you but the old woman seems to me anecdotal, in contrast to the other story. Something like the old woman was necessary. But what she causes is bigger than her. The real subject of the movie, its transgression, if that's the word, is not that she is taken from the island, that she is driven out, it's this love affair. You have succeeded in filming desire between Lee Remick and Monty. This happens one time out of ten thousand. I succeeded in filming it in a movie that you have perhaps not seen, which is* India Song. *There's not a single kiss in* Wild River, *there's a bed that serves no purpose, it lasts an hour and a* quarter, it's fabulous. One has the feeling that the actors are directing, the feeling of a sort of impetus which is given once and for all to the actors after which they have only to follow its course. The desire is never completed, never fulfilled, even when he says to her, "We're going to get married," when he is in bed, when he has just been beaten. Even at that moment there is no kiss. I saw the movie three times, and three times I felt the same amazement.

—Indeed, they never kiss.

—It's fabulous. You are perhaps the only author who has made a movie—in America—on desire, which is the unfilmable thing.

—It's difficult to film. It's not a matter of nakedness or nudity. It's important for me, I have felt it, therefore. . . . In any case, Lee Remick is one of my favorite actresses, she's a marvelous, awesome woman. Montgomery Clift was ill at that time, he had just had that horrible accident.

—Yes, he has a kind of facial paralysis which abounds in that type of timidity, of softness . . . he gives the impression of being impotent in the movie. And at that moment, impotence takes on huge proportions, becoming the main seductive appeal.

—You mean that Lee Remick awakens him, permitting him to get over that impotence?

—Oh no, on the contrary, I think Lee Remick is in love with this seductiveness, with this impotence. She breaks with heterosexual radicalism, she is in love with a man who apparently is incapable of penetrating her. That's the way I feel it, the way I see the movie.

—Yes, it's true. He was a sick man, tired, ruined, who depended at night on a nurse to watch over him. It's absolutely true, it's the truth.

—It's magnificent to have shown him. He's portrayed as he really is. It's not tragic. Or, if you will, it is tragic, but elsewhere, not in the movie. In the movie it's like a new condition of man.

And the woman completely subscribes to this new condition of man. This couple is the most truthful you could see because the brutality, the . . . It's difficult to talk about these things, to name them. Let's say that there's a constant and deadly finality in heterosexuality. And here, it is avoided. Here, I have the impression that the couple in Wild River *is united forever. It's not only a question of a marriage but of a sexual complicity from which there ensues another complicity, this one being very deep, basic, indestructible, always new because it's always risky, never certain, wandering, which will never be pinpointed and which therefore will never be pinned down and which is therefore closest to desire, to the undefined invasion of the body, of the mind by an original desire, and also the closest to the indefiniteness and to the vastness of its outcome. To tackle this is to set out on a journey. The penetration alone of woman by man, which has produced all humanity, is nothing but the procreative act, foreclosed, fixed upon itself.*

—Both of them have an enormous need for one another in the movie, for opposite reasons. Montgomery Clift was a tragic man. He was homosexual but he had a great need for women. He used to run after my first wife all the time. When I'd come home, he'd be sitting on the floor and my wife would be on the sofa. . . .

—*I don't see homosexuality as a difference. I see it as a more roundabout way. I don't see it as a problem in itself, nor female homosexuality either.*

—He had the impression that because of his homosexuality he was in an inferior position in American society. At that time there was no base of self-respect for a homosexual in Hollywood. People like John Wayne were contemptuous. The director Howard Hawks was very contemptuous. They would nail him to the wall all the time. He was trembling almost all the time. He would really tremble. I had to hold his hand in order to calm him.

—I hope there will be more trembling men like him. That word, trembling, is beautiful. Do you agree with what I've said about Wild River?

—Yes. It's one of my favorite movies. Something wasn't right in the character of the old woman. Maybe she's not down to earth enough, I don't know. For me she represented an inner strength but maybe I ought to have shown her working, to have given her more roots. She looks like she arrives on the scene with a pre-set attitude. I hadn't thought about what you said, Marguerite, about the love story between the two, but I agree. I would have said that this need they had for one another had that power because they were opposites. He was weak and distant; she brought her strength. Need met need. I've noticed in my life, I've had the experience, that when need meets need, it's what is the strongest. It's not exactly sex, perhaps it's love, desire. . . . *Hiroshima mon amour* was magnificent. But I didn't like the other movies of Resnais as much. Are you more interested now in cinema than in writing?

—Now, I think, in the written work. . . . Since we both write and make movies, we can perhaps discuss that categorical question, that question we are always asked: writing and filmmaking. Except if it bothers you . . .

—No, it doesn't bother me at all.

—You write and you make films.

—Yes, I am now writing something for a film. About my trips back to Turkey, which we were discussing.

—Do you ever write something without making a film of it?

—I hope that what I'm doing will be a book first, that it will help me find the money for a film, but not only that. I would like it to be a book first. *America, America* is also a book.

—You haven't done a book that you haven't made into a film?

—There are three books that I haven't made into films.

—That you didn't want to make into films?

—No, because they are books. *The Arrangement* I ought not

to have made into a film. *America*, on the contrary, was always a movie in my mind, I'd see it. I then wrote a book that is called *The Assassins*, then *Axe of Love* and *The Sacred Monster*, which is a good book but I haven't made it into a movie. They are too diffuse. I think that fundamentally, for me in any case, a movie must have a straighter line, not go all over the place. When I'm writing a book, I write a little, I stop, I sleep a little, I make a detour, a picnic, I meet a girl, etc. For me that's the charm of writing, but I think that the movie must be more direct.

—*But have you already found yourself with a book, or a written work—as a rule I talk about the written work, not about the book—a written work impossible to translate into film? Not by virtue of its story but, for example, by virtue of the nature of its style?*

—I would like to write well enough for that. I have no facility with language or poetry. I have feelings that I think are poetic but I don't know how to put them into a language that makes them concrete.

—*You must beware of people who write everything with ease.*

—My style can be direct, factual. I could make all my books into movies but I don't want to do it. In any case, I would like to write better. I began to write novels when I was fifty-five. It's late in a lifetime.

—*Do you love that?*

—I love life. I am at an age where I like to be alone, I like to travel. I'm not in the work of the theater anymore, I never was really part of it but now I'm completely out of it. I want to spend my time in the country and to write every morning. It's a magnificent life.

—*You, too, write in the morning?*

—Yes, I get up at five, when it's night, and I see the sunrise. I write until noon. Then I make excuses to myself, I say, "You've earned the rest of the day, now you're free."

—*Is it a passion?*

—An obsession.

—*It's the same thing.*

—And with you?

—*It's a bit different.*

—There's a feeling I find marvelous, it's when I have several pages I like. But now, I'm going to make another film. We'll see what will happen.

—*There are books of mine which I would never make into films. You agree with me all the same that the rarest thing in the world is to do what suits you. And you make the films you want to do. The films you make are Kazan's. Many filmmakers make films which they know they shouldn't be making; they make hybrid products.*

—I agree, there are some filmmakers who are dishonest.

—*Malice doesn't produce anything in cinema.*

—Their essence is not on the screen.

—*Even in good films, malice narrows the range of the film, I'm speaking of a spiritual range.*

—You are my friend from Indochina. I hadn't thought of you as coming from Indochina. You are also an immigrant, both of us are immigrants, we're lucky.

—*Yes.*

—Yes, the divided spirit.

—*Yes, not only by the distance but also by poverty in childhood. There is infinitely more variety, greater richness when all is said and done, how can I put it?—greater expansiveness, if that's the right word—in poverty than in wealth.*

—That's my opinion too.

—*The impoverished cities, the poor neighborhoods in the cities, I've experienced it in Indochina; I was on the border of Siam, we had land over there. It was a very, very poor region, and it's perhaps the happiest country I've come across in my life. The children were dying like flies, but there was a kind of force that swallowed everything, the death of the children too.*

—You must go to Turkey, you must visit the interior of the country. Have you been to India?

—*One day only. Once, when I was seventeen.*

—It's tragic. I have gone from Bombay to Calcutta twice. You must go to Turkey. I think you will understand why if you read that article in *Positif* and look at the photograph of the man in prison.

—*I've gone to Lebanon, Syria, Egypt, to Israel above all, to Greece, very, very little. It's strange, I would not have thought of going to Turkey. Are you completely or half-Jewish?*

—I'm not a Jew at all, I'm a Greek from Anatolia. My parents are Catholics, Greek Orthodox.

—*Isn't your first name, Elia, a Jewish name?*

—Elia is a Jewish first name, and Elia is a Greek first name.
—*I thought you were Jewish.*
—Oh yes, you write "Kazan, a towering figure, and a Jew."
—*He covers the planet with his films.*
—I remember, you even said: "not like Woody Allen." He's a miniaturist, isn't he? He's amusing.
—*He's a mannerist, too. There are some sublime mannerisms. For example, there is a Hollywood mannerism of the thirties, forties, or the fifties which is quite remarkable, I think—I'm not well versed in cinema. But Woody Allen's mannerism is perhaps nasty, don't you think? . . . This is fine, because it's a conversation we're having.*
—Yes. An interview is not fine; it's one against the other. I think that you're an artist, not a journalist. You write what you see.

165

—Even so, there are some things said in here, that must be kept. Are we still recording? Do I have time to talk to you about yet another thing? What I call the very, very great cinema of Kazan, I want to put it like this, like I could mention other segments from your films—the arrival in America, in America. *You film the sea, the surface of the sea.*

—Yes, it's very sad, isn't it?

—No, it isn't sad. It's New York. It's the sea which exists only there, around Manhattan.

—But so calm, it is restful. And there's a slight film of fuel oil which makes it even more calm. And the city is very far off, it haunts the spot. I adore that scene.

—It's fantastic. You film the sea three times. There's the surface with the fuel oil against the light, then you film it further on, towards the city that one almost never sees.

—Yes, the city is something that haunts one, like a ghost.

—And I think that there's a third shot. It's totally new because you haven't ever done it during the whole film and here, suddenly, you film the water, the sea, without anything else.

—What do you think of the moment when he kisses the ground?

—When he arrives in America? The whole ending is of very great beauty. It's something enormous . . . when Stavros is transformed, when he, Stavros, begins to be jealous all of a sudden. To live.

—Many of my friends told me: "For the love of God, cut that, it's so sentimental." But it is really what the people in my family felt.

—Suddenly one feels that it's a child who has been telling the story, who has been a trickster, who has been a little mythomaniac, and suddenly the whole thing comes back like youth. It has great power.

—You have a lot of power. Where does it come from? I feel it.

—*I feel something like that in me, yes.*

—Certainly. One could say that your body is full of something. Do you interpret bodies?

—*The face, yes, a lot. Gestures and the voice too.*

—All the tortures one has been through, everything one has been through, is all there, in the body. Everything that has happened to you in life is written, it can be read on you. The way one holds one's head, the way your shoulders are, and all. It's my profession too, to read this. When I was young I would always sit like this, hiding my mouth, but when I reached a certain age, I dropped my hands, and I faced the world, openly.

—*What do you call power?*

—I think it is part of desire, of the freedom to say who one is, of not being ashamed, of not hiding oneself. I think that power comes from there. For my whole life I have fought to be able to say: "I have a value and I am not going to hide what I think about anything." I used to tell myself endlessly, "Tell the truth, tell the truth." And it is difficult because the whole society, the whole culture pressures you to want to accommodate yourself to people.

—*I think that everyone has power within the self but that it doesn't always appear. I would call power the end of fear and at the same time a sort of slightly perverse attraction to truth, the slightly perverse passion for truth. And also the love of expression, the love of telling, of describing.*

—The only time in the course of the last twenty years of my life when I found myself without power was when my wife died. What I was going to do, where I was going to live, what I was going to be . . . I was shattered. But now I have to get back to normal, to find a new way to live. It's the only time this has happened to me. Aside from that, things are all right.

—*How long did you live with her?*

—Twenty-three years.

—*And what films of yours did she act in?*

—In *Splendor in the Grass* and in *Wild River*, small roles.

—*I saw Baby Doll, I haven't seen it again. Do you like it?*

—Yes. I also like A *Face in the Crowd*. I like all my films except *The Man on a Tight Rope* and *Sea of Grass*. I don't much like *Gentlemen's Agreement*, I don't know why.

—*I must be in New York from February to March.*

—You'll call me? We'll have dinner? In a Greek restaurant. . . .

—*I know only one person in New York who works in movies but I love her: Shirley MacLaine. I did an interview with her a year ago. We met afterwards and we were very happy to see each other again.*

—Yes, I love her too. Now you know two people. Do you like New York, the city?

—*I think it's the most beautiful city in the world but when I'm there I'm always at cocktail parties, evening parties . . . so this time I'm going to stay with a friend. I promised to go to his place because I no longer wanted to be there like before. I went there too often and I was completely fed up with it, always the same hotel, the same room, the same journalists. But now I'm going to stay with this friend whom I love.*

—Are you afraid of being mugged in New York?

—*Yes, I'm very afraid.*

—My wife was mugged three times, even in front of our house. They grabbed her purse, pulled, pulled her, she was very strong; they pulled her up to the street corner, they broke her fingers to get hold of her purse. They got away in a car and she, with her broken fingers, hailed a taxi, climbed in and said to the driver: "Follow that car." He replied: "You think I'm crazy?," stopped and made her get out.

—*I remember that I'd walk around New York wearing diamonds and friends told me: "Don't you see that's not a good idea?"*

168

—With all that, when I go from my house to my office every day, I see three or four interesting, stimulating things, good for books, good for movies, every day. For me, it's a necessary city. I cannot live somewhere else.

—*That's it, to live somewhere.*

—I don't have a choice. Here, the room in which M. Dauman put me costs $200 a day, it's crazy. When I'm alone in Paris and I'm the one who is paying, I go to the Hôtel de l'Odéon and when I look out the window it's like a show, like the circus; people shouting all night. I love that section of Paris.

—*This year I think I'm going to stay at the seashore. I have an apartment that overlooks the sea, the Channel. I've put in heating. It's an old mansion with ninety-two rooms and I am alone. That is, we are alone because I am rarely completely alone even so.*

—And that's where you first saw *Wanda?* At Deauville?

—*Yes, I'd seen* America *in a movie theater.* Wild River *I'd seen twice on television, and the third time I saw it in Deauville. I think it's a pity to see it on television. I need to know quite a number of things about Barbara Loden. I would like to have your opinion and Barbara's about the fact that this magnificent movie wasn't a success.*

—Barbara was very bitter, but not so much about that. The movie had been very well received by intellectuals in England and here, and in spite of this she never had the money for her later projects; that hit her hard in her life. She had things ready. For example, she wanted to make Wedekind's *Loulou.* She had a script all ready but no money. She had a script on a movie star (*A Movie Star of My Own*) that in my opinion was very good, but no money. She always had the impression that she was knocking on doors that wouldn't open.

—*Yes, but why that movie which ought to have been a success. . . . You have in America, even so, since my movies are handled*

169

like that, Godard's movies too for a long time have been handled like that. Even so, you have networks of film libraries, film clubs, don't you?

—In the universities, yes. But the movie didn't run anywhere else. Finally, she went off to the universities to give lectures with the film. She would answer questions after the showing, she would sell herself along with the movie. In this way she went to numerous colleges, in the South, in the West. She was very proud of this. She owed this only to herself, therefore she was very proud of it.

—How long ago did she do that?

—In 1971. The shooting lasted seven weeks; it was in Pennsylvania. I was there, I directed the extras, I stopped the cars from going by, etc. And I'd take care of the children.

—Do you think it would serve a purpose if I were to take a part of the script? Do you advise me to read the Wanda *script?*

—I don't think so. I'll give it to you if you wish but I think it's preferable to only see the movie. She changed the script every day. First I was the one who wrote the script, then it was like a favor I was doing for her, to give her something to do. And then she rewrote, rewrote, rewrote it, and it really became her script and not mine. It became her script. And every day during the shooting she would transform it again.

—You work like that, too, don't you?

—Yes, it's the only way. The script is not the movie.

—Yes, but it bears witness to the movie all the same.

—You know what all the good directors do, they go out in the morning, they look at the landscape, this, that, the sun. . . .

—Does Diamantis have photos of this movie?

—I think he has everything. In any case, I'm going to arrange that tomorrow. It's very important for me, for her memory.

—For me, too. I'm very intent on getting Wanda. *It's intolerable that it didn't work out at the time I had done the first release*

for Paulo Branco. They weren't able to get the movie and they had forgotten to write down its title.

—The movie was scorned in America, except in New York.

—*Do you want to talk a little about America? May I ask you some questions?*

—Yes, all you want.

—*If you were asked to sum up in several words the essential difference you see between America and Europe . . . ?*

—America remains chaotic, it's a society that is changing all the time. In New York we now have not only the blacks, but 1,250,000 Puerto Ricans who are struggling for their identity, for work, for housing. It's very difficult. Suddenly a half-million Cubans arrived in Miami, people who left because they couldn't bear life over there. The young turn against the old, scorning their parents. Here in Europe things seem to me much more settled. I've often had the impression in Greece and in France that most people are cousins; they look so much alike.

—*But don't you think that the real political happening is European? The real political events of worldwide importance originate here.*

—I think that the most intelligent and the most responsible politicians are in Europe. I have always had the impression that American politicians are way behind them. They are very pleased with themselves. It's a pity. In my life I have known two presidents, Roosevelt and Truman, who were men of a certain greatness. Roosevelt but also especially Truman. But since then, even Kennedy, whom I didn't much like, we've had very few examples of real leadership. America, on the contrary, is frozen. Europe has had cement poured over it. Even the younger generation, say in England, is beginning to rebel, but at thirty-two youth is over, it's part of the establishment. I don't know what happened here after May '68. Probably the same thing, they completely became prisoners.

171

—In any case, it was a very significant thing. It's not a question of success or failure. Politically, it is perhaps one of the three major dates of the century.

—How do *you* see the difference between America and France?

—I don't see any essential difference. I see them connected. Things happen here and are echoed in America. People leave here and America is the place they go. But I see America as a place one passes through, as a channel for what's happening in Europe, that is, for what's happening of importance on an international scale. For two centuries it's here that things have been happening. In America nothing happens but the capitalist happening, which is a happening that covers decades and decades. But I do like this idea of seeing them as complementary because America's anger is France's anger; they are mutual, violent, terrible . . . but alike. We are Europeans. I was terribly anti-American during Vietnam, of course, like the whole world.

—We were too.

—Of course. I see this in the end as fraternal anger, in view of the number one danger now which is totalitarianism, no, Soviet fascism. . . . There is a new fraternity, things are clearer.

—Have you seen my movie *The Visitors?*

—No.

—I would like you to see it.

—My son adores that movie.

—It's the first movie on Vietnam, long before the others and the best. It's very simple, very pure, like *Wanda.* If you like *Wanda,* you will probably like this movie.

—Why have we waited so long in France to see your movies?

—Because four of my movies were not at all well received in America. That made me furious. I said: "Too bad for them, shit, I'm going to write books," and I began to write books which have had some success.

—We've been waiting for America for ten years. . . .

—I made four movies that were not successful. *America, America*: a disaster and a very bad press. *The Arrangement* they made fun of in the newspapers. *The Visitors* they hooted in the theater the night of the premiere. It made me furious. I told myself, "I'm not going to stand for this much longer; why continue to make movies if people react like this? They can go to the devil!" Then there's another movie I made, a very good movie, and they were against that too. I said, "Too bad!" *The Last Tycoon* isn't a chef d'oeuvre but it's a worthy movie. I was furious with these people, I began to write, I had pleasure doing it, and there you are. But now I feel better and I'm going to start over again. I don't have a choice in any case, I must finish these five stories. *America, America*, the next one is called *The Unredeemed*, then *Anatolia*. I have no title for the fourth, and the fifth is *The Arrangement*. Five stories on my family, Greeks from Anatolia, their problems when they arrived in America. I'm going to write the story of the war of 1919–1922 which was a war in which England, France, and America forced the Greeks to fight the Turks and then betrayed them. They really and truly betrayed and abandoned them over there; it's one of the shameful effects of that war. I'll tell about the destruction of Smyrna. There it is, that's what I'm working on. I write in order to make movies, at any rate I'm going to start making movies again.

—Wanda *is a movie about "someone." Have you ever made a movie about someone?*

—I made a movie about my uncle—*America, America*. The whole family is there.

—*By someone I mean someone taken by himself, who has been considered in himself, pulled out of the set of social circumstances in which he was found. Taken out of society by you and looked at by you. I believe there is something that always remains in the self, in you, that is untouched by society, something inviolable, impenetrable, and decisive.*

—But this next movie I would like to do would get closer to that. What do you mean by "being Jewish"?

—*Because of your wandering, those bonds of wandering you have with Europe and those countries we call Turkish, Greek, Anatolian, etc. Those Mediterranean and Atlantic crossings, that wandering curve. The diaspora is not only the exodus of the Jews, it is also the presence of the Jews in their very exodus. The Jews are people who leave and who in leaving carry off with them their native land, and for whom it is more present, more violent than if they had never left it: this is what I call the wandering curve.*

—In that case, I too am a Jew.

L'HOMME ATLANTIQUE

I asked the newspaper *Le Monde* to give me some space to talk about my latest movie, *L'Homme atlantique*. It seemed to me that if I agreed to have such a movie shown, even in a single theater, I was obliged to warn people about the nature of this movie, to advise some to completely avoid seeing *L'Homme Atlantique*, even to shun it, and others to see it without fail, not to miss it on any pretext, seeing that life is short, goes by in a flash, and that the movie is going to be shown perhaps for only a couple of weeks. At the same time, I remind everyone that the major part of this movie is composed of darkness. It is customary for the majority of moviegoers in France to take cinema for granted and to protest and yell bloody murder against movies · which they consider have not been made for them alone.

I would therefore like to tell these viewers not to go into the theater showing *L'Homme atlantique*, to tell them that it isn't worth the trouble because this movie was made in total ignorance of their existence and that by going to see it they would make the potential audience of this movie uncomfortable. I therefore say to them: don't risk having to walk out, don't go. I also say this for the benefit of a great number of the journalists who take no notice of my movies, who don't think themselves obliged to come, who think it isn't worth the trouble of writing articles that take away all desire to go to movies and to read newspapers, and which harm *them*, these journalists. You will tell me that all the emotions—love, hate—vented or expressed on the showing of a film, are not the author's concern and I can tell you that people have been saying this for such a long time that it's probably wrong. If it were up to me, I would close the doors of the Escurial after the audience went in.

Safety rules prohibit my doing this. So I ask certain moviegoers not to go into the Escurial Theater when the lights are out and *L'Homme atlantique* is on. Just have them drop it, forget it. I still have this to say, that I chose the Escurial as opposed to those movie houses with mini-screens which are death, the "supermarket" houses that are taking over all of France, because the darkness of *L'Homme atlantique* must be able to be seen and looked at on the surface of a real movie screen.

This is the case here. The wonderful Escurial cinema is located at 11, boulevard de Port-Royal. Les Gobelins is the subway stop. The number 27 and 91 buses go there too. The shows run from eight o'clock to midnight. The movie is forty-five minutes long. Tickets cost fourteen francs. In the lobby of the theater, you'll see unpublished texts on *L'Homme atlantique*. If you ask me: wouldn't *L'H.A.* also be a man? I would say yes, it's also a man, but he isn't the first man because the first man doesn't exist. Would he be a man rising from the waters of the sea and who would still bear this name, Atlantic? Or would this be the name of the film? I would say yes to everything, to all the questions. That it's a man, that it's a film, that it's a film of cinema, and maybe even more, more a kind of cinema than a particular film, yes, and maybe the cinema.

FOR JULIETTE, FOR THE CINEMA
(*Libération*, October 1983)

I hadn't been to the movies for a long time. I wanted to see *Le Destin de Juliette (Juliette's Lot)* because someone had told me: "*Go, you must see it.*" Someone I believe in. And then I found that people were praising this movie in a way that discouraged me from wanting to see it. And then Aline Isserman herself talked about it on television. It was then, when I saw that she, the author, was unable to talk about it in a way that would sell it, then I went. I saw it and now it's my turn to try to sell *Le Destin de Juliette* here. Because it's a movie that you think you have time to see and that's wrong. It is in danger of disappearing, of being picked up by the hearse of mass distribution.

From the very first shots, the movie gives the impression of being unusual, different. The beauty of the direction and of the photography is such that it could be a drawback as an end in itself. And then, no. The beauty also is such that you forget about the beauty, that it's therefore playing its part, that it is inseparable from the emotion, that it *is* emotion, from beginning to end.

There's no point in telling the story; you cannot tell a story of that order. Let's say that what we have here is a terrible story, that it is lived very intensely and, at the same time, a very mysterious, secret story, from its start to the end of its journey. Isserman's movie is the story of someone who didn't die from living, who has lived a life so bare—both in hope and in despair, in railroad stations, and in seedy, grim housing projects, along the railroad tracks, and in the treeless plots of wheat fields, through zones, men, factories—that between the dreadful life of the body that goes through the horror and the life of the mind that discerns this and protects the body from it there is no difference.

177

The horror here is everywhere, seemingly everywhere, for you, for Juliette, for me. It comes naturally. It is there, it is the rain the way it is injustice, the way it is time, it is the thread of everyday life, of all existence. How, every day, every night, to avoid being killed by this man? Here is the immediacy of Juliette's life. How to hold onto life, this splendor; here are the distant thoughts of Juliette, of which she is unaware, she who is dazzling in this unawareness. Opposite her is this man who lives a parallel existence in the horror he and she share: how to avoid killing her, loving her, she, the murderess? How to avoid love, this splendor. In the middle of the movie is the child of the trinity who watches.

The phenomenal power of the film comes from this, that no one can condemn anyone. There is no cause to plead, the events are almost silent, there are cries, words too, but especially the child's. It takes place now, between 1960 and 1980, in our time. It's a glorious, almost religious film, which celebrates both the quality of innocence and of goodness, without which evil could not be inscribed, could not be written.

Four people worked on the film: Aline Isserman, Laure Duth-illeul, Dominique Le Rigoleur, Dominique Auvray. Women. Intelligent to the point of having respect for talent and for passing it on at all costs by intelligence. To the point of knowing that talent is tiresome if it says nothing, and that intelligence is never tiresome, never. And that intelligence, everywhere, in cinema too, is knowing that there is no true subject, however thin it might appear at first sight, but that which touches on all subjects and which summons the mind to seek and to find—perhaps yes, perhaps no—which subject, among all of them, is that of the film. I take my hat off to you, Laure Duthilleul, you're brilliant.

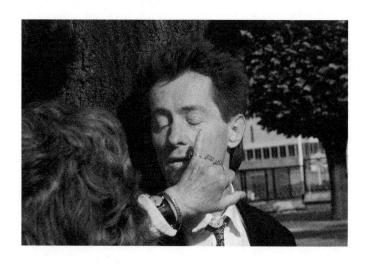

180

IN THE GARDENS OF ISRAEL,
IT WAS NEVER NIGHT
(*Cahiers du Cinéma*, July–August 1985 *)

Cahiers. *What is the genesis of* Les Enfants † (The Children)?
Marguerite Duras. My reading of Ecclesiastes when I was eighteen. Recommended reading by that little Jew of Neuilly—again and always—who became vice-consul of France in Bombay, who became the model of modern intelligence, of political despair.

—*He would shoot at the lepers?*

—Almost. He could have. But in France there were none. You know, it doesn't take much to construct a model, to get going, to press on. A sentence, a look. Here, it all started with that reading when I was eighteen. It was first called *Ernesto* in all innocence, and then *Les Enfants d'Israel (The Children of Israel)*, and then *Les Enfants du roi (The Children of the King)*. And then *Les Enfants*.

For Ecclesiastes was the king of Israel. You can't go any further than this text. It is frightful. In the movie, Ernesto was supposed to read passages from Ecclesiastes, but it is unreadable in French. Because of the repetitions, the litany.

—*The words "Vanity of vanities, all is vanity . . ." are never spoken.*

—They were.

—*Why? You took them out? Was it fear of implying too much?*

—No, it isn't that. There was no place to come back to her. They were two in the garden. He had no more time to talk about

* Interview produced by Pascal Bonitzer, Charles Tesson, and Serge Toubiana, July 1985.

† Movie adapted from *Ernesto,* a book for children written many years earlier by Duras. The movie won first prize for best script at the 1985 Berlin Film Festival.

her and there were no more pictures of him. I could have given you that long passage on the Church which was cut, only it has nothing to do with your magazine. (Laughter.)

—*Read it to us.*

—He said:

"The gardens of Israel were bathed in a violent light and it was never night.

"From that time on I lived in that light, in its bedazzlement.

"By that word he meant another word which wasn't familiar to him, but which he knew existed.

"And with that other word he no longer understood anything.

"For some time he grieved.

"For the plagues.

"For hunger.

"For the wars. The mass for the dead. Thought.

"At night he grieved. Death.

"God. He longed for God.

"Lovers he longed for.

"Adultery. And dogs and the sky. And the summer rains.

"Childhood he longed for.

"And also not knowing whom to insult, to love, to protest.

"And to know it.

"He acquired the burning desire to live without life. A life of stone, for example, or of dregs.

"Then once he did not grieve."

—*At what moment was it decided that that child would be forty?*

—As soon as they decided that it would be him. Because he was like that. In any case, at the beginning, it was Lonsdale,* you see. . . . Let's not forget how painstakingly they looked for an actor. It's awesome. I'm not saying the names of the actors

---

* Michael Lonsdale played the French vice-consul of Lahore in Duras' *India Song*.

they saw, but in theory, it was Lonsdale who was supposed to do the principal part. You see, one recognizes the vice-consul. The way one recognizes the pathways of prehistory. We did numerous try-outs on video. I myself did some for the part of the mother, but that didn't go well. There wasn't that presence, the slowness of Tatiana who is extraordinary. All the adult children didn't work either. And then all of a sudden, we thought of Axel Bougousslavsky who was our friend, Jean Mascolo's friend. We did a try-out. It was immediate. He's so innocent in what he does that the innocence is *in* him, indestructible. He has something divine, I must say. It goes so far that I thought of him to read the text of *La Maladie de la mort (The Malady of Death)*.

—*For the theater?*

—Yes, but in France. But it isn't settled yet. It's settled for Berlin, in the admirable translation by Peter Handke. I read the text in French to Peter Stein and to Luc Bondy the way I understand it is read in German; they were in agreement. It will be without pictures, it will truly be *text spoken to be seen*, nothing more. Handke's film is not only the text of *La Maladie de la mort*, it's also a text by Handke, by René Char, and by Maurice Blanchot. As far as I'm concerned, the text would be read on stage and people would listen to it. The big problem is to "strip" the place clean, to scour away anything associated with reading the text, to hear it every night with new ears. In France, I thought of Axel for the first reader. It will take someone who feels only the resonance of words, who turns a deaf ear on their allusive implications, their communicative range. Contrary to what is believed, there is no cause to plead in *La Maladie de la mort*. Nothing is hidden, there is a permanent doubt, a point of doubt that is reached and which, once reached, is subsequently never abandoned. That point of uncertainty turns precisely on the word. The book is made of words being tried out. We could only try to do this book. It isn't done, it will never be done by anyone. In its present state it is at the height of disequilibrium.

And yet, curiously, it gives the impression of being indestructible.

—*I was surprised when I met Handke at Cannes before the showing of his film. I told him that the text addressed homosexuality. He was completely taken aback.*

—Like Blanchot. It depends on the person, it would seem.

—*Still, there is at least one passage that is explicit on the subject. When it talks about "loving the bodies of those like you." He translated this text, but he didn't see it. It's amazing.*

—In *La Maladie de la mort*, the women don't spit on the men like in Handke's film. That never happened in the book. The woman smiles and sleeps, she is with the sea, she is part of the outdoors, for the time being a confined outdoors. He hasn't treated her like this but like a woman with full rights and privileges.

—*Even if he films her in little pieces, and very close up. (Laughter.)*

—In the analysis of the text of *La Maladie de la mort* one often confuses desire with sentiment, love. Now in the case of the man, one can't speak either of desire or of love. You often see that it's a man with a woman like everywhere else.

—*It's a negative reading.*

—Yes, it's a negative reading. The point of uncertainty that I reached in *La Maladie de la mort* is this: is heterosexuality the sole criterion of passion and of desire? Suddenly I doubt it. I can't say anything beyond this doubt, but I can hear in the distance the words I am not saying, that others say. When a man says he doesn't know a woman, I understand him to say that even as he's penetrating the woman, he doesn't experience that penetration as a coming together of act and thought.

—*I understand Handke's and Blanchot's oversight in the sense that we're talking about a homosexual insofar as there is a separation from women which all men may feel, even those who don't practice homosexuality.*

—Whereas there would be no separation in homosexuality. It is *oneself*. Moreover, most of the time, it's resolved like that, *oneself through oneself*. From this point of view, Handke still saw it like a romantic. Unlike woman. Now that women play with their cards on the table, this romanticism has disappeared and one very often has the feeling that they aren't there anymore, that the streets are deserted by women. Replaced by other, more literal, more direct, more dishonest women. Woman is much more complicated than what these young women think.

—*Why more dishonest?*

—Because of that immediacy of desire. Nowadays, one makes love behind the scenes, on the ground, everywhere. It's a fad, that's all.

—*Handke's perspective of the film is that of reader-translator. The title is not the right word but a word out of place. Das Mal des Todes means the stigmata of death, the mark, the stain of death.*

—I thought that it was sickness, like the sickness of living, wickedness, the devil. He avoided passages like the one with the gulls who, at dawn, start over again to gorge themselves with silt worms, to beleaguer the sands. What he has done is not a translation of the book, it's an appropriation. The film is superb. The images are magnificent. But it isn't necessarily because they are that way in the book, it's Handke who makes them this way.

—*Can we talk about* La Douleur (The War)? *I remember your mentioning at the time of* Les Yeux verts (Green Eyes) *that Gestapo agent who was more or less in love with you. In the prefatory remarks at the head of each part of your book, notably in the one entitled "Monsieur X, here known as Pierre Rabier," you say that this text doesn't join mainstream literature.*

—No, it doesn't join mainstream literature, unlike the first *La Douleur*.

—*Why? Are the events it treats less significant, not as far-reaching?*

—No, it's because *La Douleur* came out of me, out of me the way it came out of events, out of the war, out of Nazism, and all that expanded, as in the overall plan of Hiroshima, until the last sentence of the very narrative in *La Douleur:* We are all responsible for Nazism, for the dead. I give solutions in the prefatory remarks but that takes nothing away from the reading. I was told never to do this but I always do. In *Les Enfants*, I did it. I told what was going to happen to Ernesto, well before the end. In *Hiroshima* too. In *India Song* all the time; she is dead when the narrative begins. My films are backwards. All of a sudden I stop and I say that she has been buried on the banks of the Ganges. Sometimes I unveil destiny by putting events in the future perfect. "She would have been beautiful," "she would have swum far. . . ." In such a way that the present partakes of the end, of death, that it is stamped by it.

—Is there some reason why La Douleur *appeared when it did? I thought of those words you had said in your interview with Pivot where I had the feeling that you were putting everybody in the same bag—collaboration and Stalinism—whereas today, after* La Douleur, *you are completely reopening the wound.*

—I had promised a text to P.O.L. because he had published texts that the other publishers had rejected. In particular, texts by Leslie Kaplan, that little Jew from New York who is now one of the greatest French poets. She wrote: *L'excès, l'usine, Le Livre des Ciels, Le Criminel.* She's magnificent. P.O.L. is a very careful reader. It was very difficult to remember Leslie as she went by, to see what was outstanding in the waves of her books. P.O.L. saw it.

About the coming out of *La Douleur*, Barbet Schroeder told me: "*La Douleur* after *L'Amant (The Lover)*, if it isn't planned, it's brilliant, if that's what it was, it would be too much." I didn't want it. I was late for P.O.L.'s book; he wanted to bring it out before the summer, I thought about nothing else but this delay. The critics were sometimes enthusiastic about *La Douleur*, sometimes shocked. There was someone at *La Quinzaine littéraire* who reproached me for having written it. The argument was that with Le Pen around, this wasn't the moment to recall a man being tortured. I was quite in despair, I wasn't sorry at all of course, simply sorry that in a newspaper like *La Quinzaine* one could make arguments of that kind, of simple convenience, of literary strategy. There are people who have spoken of *La Douleur* as if it were a tremendous love story. Who understood that it was unbearable. It turned out that all these people were young, no old ones.

—One gathers from the reviews that it's something other than literature. I find, on the contrary, that it's the highest form of

187

literature because the writing captures something impossible to evoke and the text manages to do it, particularly through that whole shitty story. I remember another version which appeared in Sorcières.

—Here it's the complete version, the one in the war note-books. The other version was very short, three pages, the one that appeared in *Sorcières*. It's a difficult text. It's hard to be in a needless repetition, that litany of sorrow which is almost always paroxysmal, unbearable. In *L'Amant*, I had several very harsh reproaches from Jews about the sentence on the execution of Brasillach: "Why did you say that (that he talked but that he would not have done any harm)? You shouldn't have." I would ask them: "What should I have done then? Kill him?" They don't say yes. They don't say no. That's some improvement. Should I have killed him? They don't answer, they say: "You shouldn't have said that he shouldn't be killed."

—You followed that business about a film on the Manouchian group, Des Terroristes à la retraite (The Retired Terrorists): *those judges convened by the Communist Party in order to say what it was. It's odd, I think that young people cannot understand that you have to get that whole machine of heroic figures moving in order to invoke the truth. The difference is that with your book one is thrown into it. The scene in the restaurant with Rabier and the other couple, that's cinema. We are in the picture. Far from history, from the official lie.*

—What I took out is on the Catholics. I was denying Catholics the same capacity for suffering from that terrible hatred which was only ours, women's. The priest who brought back the German orphan, I kept him. We were against him. What is this unscrupulousness released from our criminal instinct? We had to go through crimes, we wanted to kill the Germans, we wanted to exterminate them. That had to be respected too. That was part of us, of the suffering. That hatred was to be respected. I see it all again very well. The truckloads of women waiting for night to come. The searchlights. I still hear my footsteps in la rue des Saints-Pères when I go away.

—The book is at the same time an extraordinary catalog of bodies, of the physical types that emerged from that period, from those in La Douleur *to the body of the young militiaman who handed over the Jews.*

—I changed almost nothing. It's neo-realist like the literature of that time. But not *La Douleur*. There the reality is so awful that it is unrealistic. The repetition of one day after another, the sameness of the suffering, the poverty of the language describing it, reaches a depth by itself.

—Being a Communist, how could you desire a militiaman?

—You are capable of everything. Desire is capable of everything. It was desire like any other one, fleeting, common, but which went looking far afield, to where it was forbidden. I remember it only because it was recorded in a written work—and this because it was a criminal object of desire. Without this it would have been forgotten.

—*Do you imagine what you're asking of the reader, to go from* L'Amant *to* La Douleur?

—*La Douleur* was called *La Guerre (The War)*. It was broader.

—*There are many people who discovered you with* L'Amant.

—There are many people who are discovering me with *La Douleur*. It's probably here that I have belonged to this country, with the war in all of Europe, not before then, except through reading. Yes, I think so.

—*I listened to* La Masque et la Plume (The Mask and the Pen). *The professionals of literature and criticism don't believe in the device: "I wrote this long ago and I rediscovered it in a wardrobe." They think you've cheated.*

—I didn't cheat about the suffering. What do you want? I cheated about the Catholics. I'm talking about *La Douleur*, about *Albert des Capitales (Albert of the Capitals)*, and *Ter le Milicien (Ter the Militiaman)*. Rabier was written recently but equally from numerous notes. I can show the notebooks. I can show the notebooks. I don't know anymore where I wrote them. I must have kept the newspapers in order to quote the articles the way I do. That is certain. But where was it? In the deportees' homes? And when? When I was sure that Robert L. would live, that's for sure. Maybe it's after that vacation in '46? In the same notebooks, I rediscover the first drafts of *Un Barrage contre le Pacifique (The Sea Wall)*, of *Le Marin de Gibraltar (The Sailor from Gibraltar)*, of *Madame Dodin*, and of endless accounts of vacations in that same spot from which *Savannah Bay* was written.

—*In the beginning, it's written somewhat in the form of a diary, but not at the end, where it's from the distant past, whereas before you feel the immediate continuity of the event.*

—In the beginning I know someone who has been deported. He was in Germany and we couldn't yet imagine what was going on in the camps. And when he returns, this man, I don't recognize him. I recognize him in the split second of a smile, then I lose him again.

I don't know by what miracle I got to the end of the book, to that end. Genius is always external, you think it's in the self but it's often from the other side that it comes. All of a sudden, in the evening light on the beach, in the peacefulness, someone, a woman, speaks of Robert L. She says that she fears he will never again be able to use his legs. She speaks of him as one would of a living being, of a child too. It's through these two sentences relating to his weakened body, his slightly hesitant walk, these two sentences heard in the evening that Robert L. comes back to life for me, that he is once again involved in life. *He* doesn't know what is happening for a moment, in the evening light, on the beach. The war ends there too. We will not live together, he and I. Because that love has already been lived out, beyond our strength.

Les Enfants. We can talk about *Les Enfants.* Unless we're talking only about books. It would be good for once not to talk about cinema. I would be delighted. *Les Enfants*, I'm going to tell you what happened. For me, cinema has gone bad. I have suffered so much for me and for my friends that the film is a bit spoiled.

—*To talk like Ernesto, do you think that the film, the whole thing, wasn't worth the trouble?*

—Yes, it was worth the trouble. It will come back to me. Already I'm more willing to talk about it but up to this point, it was dreadful because of the conditions of production. But I've already talked about that a little in *Libération.*

—*And that child, didn't he experience the events we were talking about earlier?*

—No. The others, in comparison with him, are quite young, of average size. His sister is likewise seven. Why seven? It's a convenience the parents allow themselves in order not to withhold the age of their children: they are all seven.

—*With the scene of the potatoes, at the end, one thinks of the bread and wine of the Sacrifice.*

—I hadn't thought of it.

—*There's that final shot that sweeps the garden, the empty armchairs, a gate. You almost have the impression of seeing the absence of God.*

—Even so, I had talked to the actors a little about what Ernesto's suffering was but without specific directions. I found that at the end, when they are talking about God and about science, they do it with tremendous tact. Without any shade of mockery, whereas, two minutes before, they were so given to wild laughter that we had to cut. Here, no, they came together in seriousness. But Ernesto is not going to die of God. It's true that I wasn't able to say it at the end. It's in the shot where I'm talking over his face, in the garden of the school, that I tell what he will become, that he's leaving for America, etc. After the scene of the meal, at the end, I can no longer say anything more about him. Or else the balance would have been wrong.

—*The comedy in the film is very cinematographic, very visual. If in a book you say that Ernesto is seven and that he looks like forty, that won't be the case for André Dussollier, who has the actor who plays Ernesto in front of him and who says to him: "All right, what do you say. . . ." How did you work with the actors during the shooting?*

—When Ernesto was alone talking with his mother, they were listening. They were all there. The film was shot chronologically. We couldn't do it any other way. We were in complete agreement on the shooting, it was brilliant. The idea was perhaps brilliant and he is even more so. He's Russian-Polish. It's true he looks like Stan Laurel. In *Les Enfants*, compared to my previous films, there's an abstract element that is dropped. It comes from the three of us having worked together. I would suggest things and they would tell me what they thought of them. Now and then, they would suggest others. Sometimes, we would all reject the way the film was going, the writing itself. Occasionally it was the opposite, they would suggest and I would reject. They were always afraid because they knew me, that I would drop the comedy of the film in the first of the six versions of the script that we had done for l'INA.* My son thought that the part of Gélin was too talkative, completely silly. He was right. He was also the one who made me cut the shot of the church by twelve minutes. On one hand, there's the house, on the other there's the school, and between them is that intemporal place that is the court. Ernesto's face replaced the church. It's over this face that I tell what his life has been like.

—Les Enfants *is an easier film than the others but it's no less dense and mysterious. It's simple only on the surface. Like Ernesto who is a disarming and very complex character.*

—There are some things that are shocking, the ones that come from the other side of the self. Later, you notice that you had not intended them. Like my brother's maleficence in *L'Amant*. Like God, here, in *Les Enfants*. My two co-authors accepted it. Religion I didn't talk about. I'm talking about it now. I don't believe in God. I am the way I was at eighteen, exempt from any faith.

—*Is there a gap? It's the film's subject.*

—Between death and eternal life, the expansion of life's range must be unbearable. The believers never talk about it. We know nothing about someone who is a believer, never. I don't know Ernesto. All I do is listen to him. I don't know if Ernesto

* L'Institut National de l'Audiovisuel, an archive of film footage.

believes in God. I think that having to settle it without making up his mind tortures him, that this is where he is.

—*Ernesto is very different from the people who today reject knowledge.*

—He doesn't have fashionable ideas. He has no recipes, no principles, no morals.

—*It's Ernesto's sentence that makes him famous throughout all France: "I don't want to go to school because I am taught things I do not know." Would you say that he's a saint?*

—No, I would say that he is in contradiction. That humanity has lost him and that he is its greatest loss. That he sticks to what he knows just as to what he doesn't know. That he constantly talks about God. Like me who doesn't believe in him. That the word is here for the two of us but that it's Ernesto who uses it with full rights and privileges. A saint? No. He does not lie, he doesn't hide. Anything. He's a child: if he had in his hands news about the end of the world, he would spread it like news of a holiday. I feel him to be very close to death.

—*The actor's gaze is strange. It doesn't meet people, it goes through them. Did you ask him to look like that?*

—He's like that. He must know it. The mother, she has everything in her. She cannot name what she has missed. Ernesto can.

—*And the other children alluded to in the title, don't we ever see them?*

—No, it wasn't worth the trouble. It's just believable: Ernesto is always in the midst of looking for them, for his brothers and sisters, at the Prisu store or somewhere else. He's already a pastor. He's responsible. The mother, she's the queen mother; she has abandoned her children and they understand and respect her and love her for the very fact that she was capable of doing it.

I haven't finished with literature. I am someone who writes, *first and foremost.* My involvement in cinema? I haven't been to the movies for five or six years. I see films on television. During the Cannes film festival, I see excerpts of the ones in the coming year. I believe that cinema doesn't exist anymore. Except what I call the big-run movies, the fear movies, the ones that smell bad. The problem I see in cinema, the cinema that still goes by this name—maybe you're too caught up in it to see it—is that one can go from one film to the other, leave one, find another, without noticing it anymore. The people kiss the same way, the bodies are naked the same way, the stories are the same. I don't see any difference between the people who make movies, between the actors who act in them, and between the stories that are told. It's like cellular division—one film breeds another, one face another, one fashion, one theme, etc. I was saying to Serge Daney: there's no emotion anymore, no real fear anymore, there is no anything anymore, except televised films. Lanzmann's film, what is it called? I want to see it.

—Shoah. *When you talk about the cinema, is Godard the only exception you make?*

—No, but when one feels alone and one thinks of another filmmaker, it's Godard. To see a film now is to decide to pass some time with the help of a film. It's no longer the film that determines what you are going to do with your evening. Therefore it's not cinema anymore. Perhaps some day it will be abandoned, like cars, boats, travels. This may happen after a man, on finding himself in great and terrible moral turmoil, should, just once, by chance, pick up a book, read it, and forget everything else.

—*There are, all the same, filmmakers who now and then bring good news. The malady you describe is that of the industry, which hasn't always been like this. Great films have come out of the same molds, in Hollywood and in Japan.*

—For several years, I've had the impression sometimes, and

even most of the time, that it's no longer the writers who are doing the writing and that it's no longer the filmmakers who are making the films. That it's other people. People who are not quite whole. Vague people, who don't go beyond technique, whom one doesn't know, television people perhaps, but ones from the back country, not from the coast. Bresson must have made a movie a year, I ought to make a movie a year. But there's no money for us. In our crowd, there's only Godard, Resnais, Rohmer who make a film a year and with success. Bresson's *L'Argent (Money)* was seen by fifty thousand viewers.

—. . . *and not seen by seven hundred thousand viewers who wouldn't have seen it for anything in the world.*

—Bresson is tremendous. He's the inaugurator of all of cinema. When you go to see a film by Bresson you have the feeling you've never been to the movies. When I go to see *Son nom de Venise dans Calcutta desert (Her Name of Venice in Calcutta Desert)*, I have never been to the movies before. The feeling of *the first time*, of a first love, it's gone, it's over. If the younger generation rejects Bresson, it's because they have lost their own youth, their passion.

—*And television, which in showing pictures vulgarizes them, what part does it play, in your view?*

—It is irreplaceable. It is the immediacy of information, the obliteration of distance. But it has the same defect as contemporary film: it skirts the issues—it presents things badly. It passes the time too. There's the *Chateauvallon* series which wasn't bad in the beginning but which right now is taking a turn for the worse. Four to six weeks, big things have been in the offing, but what they are you don't know. The drama, you understand, is that *they* don't know either. (Laughter.) They load it with new incidents, but don't seem to be able to come up with the consequences of these incidents. It's often like that with television and cinema, like poorly stitched clothing, where you can see the botched job, the spelling mistakes in the film. Filmmakers in general, and especially the new ones, don't read: they read scripts. Even the book they are reading becomes impoverished because they read it like a script. I know a filmmaker who reads Nietzsche. He reads to read. He is not unaware that it's by reading that one learns to work with one's head, but it must be unwittingly. That the worst kind of reading is the kind that has gone off its own track.

—*Are you aware of the proportions of what you're saying about cinema, that it will probably no longer be the popular culture that it was?*

—Yes, but less than reading. I'm going to tell you the people I ought to have liked whom I didn't like. There's nothing I can do about it. There is René Clair, that sweet, nice side I cannot bear. I've never liked Guitry either. I know now he's become fashionable. I don't like Bergman. I like Dreyer but I saw *Gertrud* again and I was terribly disappointed. Cocteau, I don't like much, no. Renoir, yes, I love. He's probably my favorite among the ones who are dead. *Le Fleuve (The River)* is superb. That child with the snake, the pictures of the Ganges. I like Ozu, Satyajit Ray, Fritz Lang, John Ford, Chaplin, and Tati. There's a filmmaker I've just discovered, it's Rouch. What he does I find brilliant. *Cocorico monsieur Poulet (Cock-a-doodle-do Mister Chicken)*. (Laughter.) This is the other language. There's the language of Rouch and the language of *Les Enfants*. You have to put them on a parallel line. Not with Godard. Not with Bresson. But with Rouch and Duras, there *is* a new language, this hybrid tongue. What a rest, what freshness.

—*Tell us, in your view, how are we going to do without cinema, without the great films?*

—We are beginning to. As proof, I take myself as an example. I watch television a lot and I don't have Canal Plus.* I don't miss it too much. Sometimes, when I see the title of

* A pay-television channel.

movies that are on, I prefer not to know them. Many of my friends see only certain things on television. *I* watch it every day. I know very well how to watch it. You learn this. When a program is rigged, you know it. It isn't only to see movies that I watch television. It's to have an up-to-date contact with my time, to be here. To have TV is to be here and be with it. To be in Beirut. For if I were the only one watching television, I wouldn't watch it. It's common information that I'm looking at, that I'm sharing. For sports, it's marvelous. For gymnastics. Tennis. With Daney, it's our meeting ground.

—*Did you see the Navratilova-Evert Lloyd finals?*

—It was sublime. What a lesson for men. Apart from Noah, suddenly there was grace in sports.

Les Enfants? Success or lack of it does not influence the artist's output. The artist's body of work survives lack of success if it deserves to be preserved. There isn't any oblivion anymore, no hell anymore for the artist's body of work. A phony painter may exist, a gallery may decide to "launch" such a painter on the international market. It's a matter of value, of monetary invest-ment—it's done all the time. But if the painter launched by the gallery is not a great painter he will not last more than twenty years. We know these figures. Truth always comes out in the end.

Les Enfants? I have to remember that this movie exists. Because it was spoiled by the conditions of production. When you struggle for ten months so that the names of your co-authors may be put in the opening credits and the producers, pretending to yield to the judge's decision, put them after the final credits, after the blackout of the final credits, almost after the curtain, just to slap you in the face, to do harm, you see what cinema has come to. They've reached the level of slime. That's where I am, as if stepping out of the slime. I must forget the strange, near-murderous rancor, the fear too, for sometimes I was afraid. I must rediscover the movie in its innocence.

198